Hearing from Wayne

AND OTHER STORIES

Hearing from Wayne

AND OTHER STORIES

BILL FRANZEN

Alfred A. Knopf New York 1988

*Most of the stories in this collection were originally published
in the following periodicals:* Gentlemen's Quarterly, Harper's,
National Lampoon, The New Yorker, *and* Soho Weekly News.

Library of Congress Cataloging-in-Publication Data
Franzen, Bill, {date}
Hearing from Wayne.
1. American wit and humor.   I. Title.
PN6162.F727   1988   813'.54   87-45260
ISBN 0-394-55501-5

Manufactured in the United States of America

First Edition

I'VE always tried to be a good driver, but now that I'm married I try extra hard, using all the recommended defensive driving techniques. It's this new feeling I have of wanting to protect more than myself. So when my wife and I made a big trip recently, I avoided doing anything like, say, tailgating. We traveled from New York to Minnesota by way of Niagara Falls, Ontario, Upper Michigan, and Wisconsin. Since my wife, Roz, doesn't drive, I drove it all. Naturally, I did all the driving on the way back, too: virtually all Interstate 80, a dull but fast way to get East. At the end of each day I would check the *Rand McNally* to see how many inches of it we'd put behind us. Now that we're back in New York and are busy again with our little routines, I miss some of that monotonous time in the car together. Even your dullest stretch has the occasional billboard. (I spotted one for Ken & Lu's Pair-A-Dice Lounge; Roz caught a sign for the Memory Lane Motel.) And of course every so often we gave our radio dial the sweep. We pulled in a lot of mom-and-pop-type stations, the kind always making predictions about things like rain (don't expect any soon); heifer prices (they'll climb slightly); and Jesus (won't be long now).

Often, though, we just sped along quietly. During one of those meditative periods—we were passing through Ohio—Roz suddenly asked, "What's the difference between concrete and cement?" That led to a long discussion filled with a lot of guesswork. And that somehow sprouted another conversation that gradually twisted and turned its way around to this weird point that had Roz, who is in the small category, physically, reassuring me that if I was ever attacked by some big guy she wouldn't act like most of the gals you see on TV shows, who all too frequently will just stand there and scream while their guys get beat up. She promised me that if we ever found ourselves in one of those bad situations, she'd take a vase or something and let the other guy have it. Well, that line of talk ended as a bank of purplish-black clouds started to commandeer the afternoon sky to the left of I-80. It looked like one heck of a storm forming. For a while we had the illusion that we could outrun it, but this was something big, right off the Great Lakes, and it spread over us until it was like a scary version of night. Roz was twisting around in her seat and taking pictures. Then, as the hot-white lightning bolts seemed to come closer and the accompanying thunder got louder, she snapped the camera back in its case and asked me if we were in any danger. I wasn't certain, but I reassured her, nonetheless, that we were quite safe. I was *pretty* sure that a car was still an okay place to be. At the same time, I was dematerializing our Honda in my mind, and pictured us sailing through Ohio, in sitting position still, and with lightning exploding around us. I felt kind of vulnerable. There wasn't much else to do, though, but grip the wheel against the wind in the recommended ten-and-two position, put the wipers on high, and drive that wicked stretch as safely as I knew how. This gal on my right was willing to pick up a vase and crown a bad guy for me, so I wasn't about to let down just then.

to Roz

CONTENTS

Contents

ACKNOWLEDGMENTS

My sincere thanks to editors
Dan Menaker, Trish Deitch Rohrer,
Adam Gopnik, and Terry Adams.

Hearing from Wayne

AND OTHER STORIES

Hearing from Wayne

WHILE I was flipping through the day's mail after a real yawn fest of a workday at the Stereo Shack, I came across something that knocked me over like a good brushback pitch. It was a postcard from Wayne, and I've really got to hand it to him, but before I get going on Wayne's postcard and on Wayne and on how Wayne was my best friend and just the whole incredible Wayne story, I'd like to say right up front that my *real* fear of any kind of hereafter is that instead of being sort of reunited with my family and friends and everyone I've ever felt close to, I'll get there and find myself in the middle of just casual acquaintances—people I recognize, people I always said hi-how-you-doing to, but *nobody* I ever felt close to. Like the guy from the luncheonette, kitty-corner from the Stereo Shack, who makes the great two-story ham sandwiches, plenty of mustard, but who I can't exactly say I'm attached to. He's a nice guy and all, and I even gave him 10 percent on some speakers once, but if he's the first person I see in the afterlife it'll be some letdown. And if I reach life's nineteenth hole *before* him, and I'm the first one *he* sees, I can understand how it'll sour the whole experience for him, too. I'd probably try to duck before he saw me, but if he saw me ducking, that would be pretty awful. I mean, imagine yourself popping through into extra innings, only to see one of your regular sandwich customers, who suddenly ducks, pretends he doesn't know you, pretends you never made maybe two hundred and ninety-seven ham sandwiches for him during his lifetime, plenty of mustard. Now, I can't tell from Wayne's postcard if the afterlife ever starts out that creepy for anyone, but if it does, it's just like Wayne not to go into it. That's the way Wayne was, and one reason why he was my best friend and one reason why he'll stay my best friend, especially if he can keep up this great second effort through the mail. He did slip in a few comments about the afterlife on his card, but nothing that would scare any of us still playing life's back nine.

On a snowy night one year ago, Wayne and I were sitting and watering our faces in that Wild West bar called the Sitting Bull. Above the bar, there's this giant painting of four Sioux Indians in big, flowing headdresses riding in a gondola in Venice that Wayne was so crazy about, and right in front of us those upside-down cowboy hats with the barbecue-flavored party mix that we both liked. Wayne and I were swapping stories about Harold, the Stereo Shack's only TV salesman and a buddy from the Stereo

Shack's softball team. Harold had recently left the team and every other earthly organization after plowing smack into an oak tree. He wasn't even supposed to be driving. This guy was a narcoleptic, which means permission denied as far as getting your hands on a wheel in this state goes. So anyway, old Wayne and I get to wondering what Harold's .450 batting average is doing for him wherever he is now, and soon we're speculating as to what that wherever actually is and if it would be possible for a guy exiting to that place to smuggle in a room equalizer. I explain to Wayne my fear of seeing just people I kind of recognize there, but take-it-as-it-comes Wayne, of course, says he's not worried, and laughs through a mouthful of party mix. He says he's expecting something more like the best room they have at the Ramada Inn in Fort Lauderdale, with telepathic models bringing you and your best deceased pals frothy turquoise drinks just as soon as you've all drained your clear orange ones.

Eventually, I get around to telling Wayne about Houdini and his wife. I took this book out from the bookmobile once that was all about the Houdinis conducting their own afterlife experiment. They went and promised each other that the first one of them to die would do everything possible to reach the one still alive. Well, Harry Houdini died in 1926. And, according to the book, before Beatrice Houdini died, in 1943, she admitted that she'd never heard from Harry and called their experiment a failure. But Wayne, who I guess was feeling his boilermakers pretty well by then, says he loves the idea anyway, and he gets me to say "What the heck" and shake hands and then sign and date a Sitting Bull Bar cocktail napkin with him to cement our own pact, and a man next to us who's been muttering something about his sister making a thousand dollars a second seems glad to sign it, too.

WELL, that was a year ago. Then, a half-year later, Wayne and I are locking up the Stereo Shack after a real gutterball of a business day when Wayne turns to me and says, "Let's call 'em." So we take turns calling our wives from a phone booth in the parking lot, and fifty cents later we're loose. There's some all-you-can-stand fish fry at the Sitting Bull, but it sounds a little too bush league to us. Instead, we drive out to Long Lake and smack two large buckets of balls each at Denny's Driving Range. Wayne uses a three-wood and after every swipe says—loud enough for everybody there, including Denny, to hear—"*That's* on the green." Then we go nearby for some Italian and a couple of pitchers of cold draft. Later, when we're cruising back in my Toronado with all the windows down, Wayne finds the head of a green toy soldier in my glove compartment. It's just this tiny little rubbery soldier head without a body that my kid, Timmy, probably left around, and it made us laugh. Then Wayne puts it in his left nostril—just a little ways—so that the little army man could sort of look out, and then turns so they're both looking at me. And that really cracks me up. Next, Wayne says something like "Eyes on the road!" and snaps his head straight ahead, so that the soldier watches the road, and it's stupid, but we're giggling like high-schoolers and tears are coming down. But then Wayne—gasping for air—sort of snorts inwards and the little head vanished and we had to drive right to Long Island Hospital and it wasn't funny anymore. And the way it turned out, the inside of that hospital was the last thing on earth poor Wayne ever saw—at least in this life.

A N Y W A Y, Wayne's postcard is a miniature version of the big painting above the bar at the Sitting Bull—the one with the four Sioux Indians in headdresses riding in a gondola in Venice. Except that on Wayne's postcard there's a fifth passenger squeezed in between two of the Indians, and it's Wayne in his Stereo Shack softball uniform, smiling and with his cap on backwards. There wasn't a stamp or a postage mark anywhere on the card, but there was a decent-sized message in Wayne's usual slanty brand of printing. Wayne began by saying hi and saying he bet I was surprised he'd got ahold of me like we'd talked about and that he missed hanging out together, but that at least this was some kind of way to reach me. Then he asked if my Timmy was still playing Battle of the Bulge in the car, and wrote "ha ha" afterwards. He said that his notion of the hereafter being something like a room at the Ramada Inn in Fort Lauderdale was way off, except for the turquoise drinks. He said that the stereo systems there aren't nearly as impressive as you might expect, but added, "The acoustics in our modules are choice." He plays a lot of what he calls Cluster Ball there—"a potent blend of golf, bowling, and softball for large numbers," in his words. Then he advised me to get out in life and shake my tail feathers all I can, and said if I wanted to perform one especially decent act, I should tell the police that seventy-nine cats and eleven dogs are being kept inside a home at 281 South Brook Lane, about half a mile from Denny's Driving Range.

Finally, Wayne said it's really not so bad after your third strike and not to worry about it but just to stay loose and go with it and that everything will make a lot more sense to me when we meet up again—"more than you could ever imagine right now," Wayne wrote. Which was nice of Wayne to say, and another reason why he was my best friend and why he'll stay my best friend—regardless of whether or not he can keep up this great second effort through the mail.

The Brewster Family
Time Capsule

W E   B R E W S T E R S   weren't   showing
much improvement, so Marv, the family counselor assigned
to us by the state, finally recommended that we try working
together on a Brewster Family Time Capsule, to be buried
in our backyard and not dug up until New Year's Day,
2001. Marv said he'd recently persuaded a family called
the Craydahls to try it; apparently, communication around
the Craydahl dinner table had dropped off to where a Craydahl was just as likely to point at another family member,
go "Blam," and then blow across the end of his finger, as
talk to that member. According to Marv, though, once
these Craydahls had settled on "certain family items,"
tucked the items into an old paint can, and hidden the can
four feet beneath the loosest block in their patio, their
dinners together began to involve so much cooing and

jabbering with their mouths full that now there's going to be a whole "Nova" episode coming out on it.

Still, we Brewsters hemmed and hawed every time Marv tried to steer us into doing our own family time capsule. Assembling one might be mildly therapeutic, sure, but it also sounded like a real hassle. And just how much would it actually say about us in 2001—in only thirteen years? Plus, none of us—not Dad, Mom, my teenage sister, Jodi, or me—was exactly wasting anyone at dinner, yet.

But then one night I blew it. While Marv was over emceeing our ninth weekly session in the living room, I let it slip that dinners at our place meant loading up a tray in the kitchen and then hightailing it to one of the far corners of the house. And boy, did news of our come-and-get-it-and-go suppers ever turn up the flame under Marv's loafers. I mean, in no time he had rolled our vacuum cleaner out into the living room and had started using it to inflate a wrinkled, flamingo-colored plastic bundle he'd pulled out of his attaché case. It expanded rapidly, pinning one poor floor lamp against a wall until the shade finally caved in and the bulb popped. Fully inflated, this plastic thing was like a gigantic pink wok. Marv called it his "dialogue pit," and he coaxed us into kicking off our shoes, diving in, and lounging around inside it with him. He said we should all just relax in its "bowlness" and start thinking out loud about what was special enough to be included in our family time capsule—bearing in mind, of course, that we'd all be showing up and opening it together in thirteen years. Marv had one ground rule, though: If *any one* of us objected to someone else's proposed item, that item was automatically out.

My sister, Jodi, a high-school senior, immediately

announced that she was putting in her Brent poster, which she keeps on the outside of her bedroom door. Brent is her considerably older boyfriend, who likes to brag that he's "taking a break from the work force." He is, too, thanks to the regular insurance checks he gets from having faked a bulldozer injury at the landfill. And I was the one out there, at what we call Mount Trashmore, driving the bulldozer at the time. I was also the fool who'd talked the Trashmore manager into hiring Brent in the first place, so now the manager has me scrambling over the swampiest part of the fill in hip boots, overseeing all incoming decaying organic matter. Anyway, the so-called Brent poster that Jodi wanted placed in our capsule included a lot of Jodi, too. It showed her in a skimpy red nightie, riding high on Brent's shoulders in our local Mardi Gras Days parade. The poster was actually a blowup of a Polaroid that a friend of Jodi's had taken. So, in the dialogue pit, it wasn't too astonishing when Mom smiled and said, "I don't *think* so, Jod," which, of course, was it for Jodi's poster right there. Just the same, Dad threw in a " 'fraid not," as if he were the one barring Jodi's poster—then added that the only Brent-related thing he'd allow in our capsule would be Brent himself. See, the folks *did* agree on Brent. They didn't care for him, partly because he'd taught Jodi to tear the filters off her Camel Lights and partly because he'd once tried using Dad's home computer to put himself on at full salary at the munitions company where Dad works as a sales rep. Anyhow, Marv finally spoke up to tell Jodi he was sorry her poster had been turned down and to ask if she'd share with us her reasons for wanting it in the time capsule in the first place. "Because in thirteen years," she said, her pupils large and mad,

"I'd like to hold it up and go 'See?' because Brent and I are *so* in love, and still *will* be in 2001."

Dad jumped in next, claiming he had a "worthy piece of hardware" for the capsule: his big wing nut from atop the mantelpiece in the den. It came off one of the old ships that had been anchored in the Pacific for an A-bomb test they'd conducted at the end of the war. One of Dad's Navy buddies had given it to him; this was a guy, the story went, who'd cruised into the bomb site with a Geiger counter twenty-four hours after the blast to study what a nuclear explosion could do at sea. One side of the recovered wing nut was still coated with paint, and the other side, the blast side, was shiny. I'd picked it up maybe once in my life; it was creepy, and had always bugged all of us except Dad. Anyway, Jodi immediately said, "Over my dead body," and that was it for Dad's wing-nut hopes. In frustration he pounded the pink plastic, and we all felt the hit through that overgrown beach toy. Marv, eager to get off Dad, gave me a little come-come-come with both hands, as if he were hurrying me into a parking space.

Well, I had to confess I was wearing what I wanted to contribute to our time capsule: my black cotton Hugh's Raw Bar T-shirt, which I'd picked up on a spring-break trip to Florida. I'd stayed way too long and ended up dropping out of college. Still, those "Hugh Brew"-and-oyster lunches, after upwards of two hours on a jet ski, were a special memory from my trip south. And you wouldn't believe how comfortable that shirt turned after a few dozen washings. Of course, it had also developed some holes, its maroon lettering had faded to pink, and both *D*'s in "Lauderdale" had come off completely, leaving me with LAU ER ALE across my chest. So I wasn't too shocked to hear Dad, Mom, and Jodi all "nay" the thing.

Next was Mom's turn, and she didn't surprise us one bit. See, her big passion is making things from ordinary household junk. She'll spend days building angels out of Styrofoam packing pellets or creating banks that resemble turtles from old margarine tubs. Once, when she ran too low on supplies, I actually had to drive out to Mount Trashmore *on a Saturday* and fill my trunk with egg cartons, bleach bottles, coat hangers, empty ham cans—you name it—just to shut her up. So sure enough, Mom wanted to put her most prized creation into our capsule: her chimes made from those skinny olive jars. They had basically ruined the front porch for the rest of us, and now it took a whole two seconds for Dad, Jodi, and me to vote thumbs down. We didn't want that earache-on-a-string taking up valuable capsule space, and besides, all *our* stuff had been turned down.

Well, before we could start over and try to agree on new items, Marv swung us into discussing something less controversial: What exactly should we use as a time capsule? Marv, fidgeting with his ID bracelet, said he had an empty typewriter case just taking up space in his apartment. None of us Brewsters expressed the slightest interest. Jodi started saying something about Brent having a U.S. Postal Service strongbox under his bed, but then she put on the brakes, erased the air in front of her with a filterless Camel Light, and said, "No, no, no, I must have dreamt that." Then Mom brought up the idea of using a flour canister that she'd found at a yard sale—it had come chock-full of wooden ice-cream spoons—and said she'd made it "real cute" by gluing tiny musical notes around it that she'd razor-bladed from the cork inside soda-bottle caps. Everyone groaned, Marv included. Dad, folding his arms across his chest, said to consider it settled: We'd use his big, shiny bullet from the den. And you know, much as we hated to give Dad his way so easily, it wasn't a bad idea. Dad's company had once displayed this big model bullet in its booth at a munitions expo—it was double the size of a thermos. And, most important, this hollow "bullet" unscrewed in the middle. So burying our stuff in there did make a lot of sense. Plus, it didn't hurt to show Marv that we Brewsters could agree on *some*thing.

Then Marv really threw us a curve. He said that since none of our time-capsule picks had received "family clearance" in the first go-round, we could, if we *all* agreed to it, lift our earlier vetoes and let everyone put in his or her original choice. That, Marv suddenly disclosed, was exactly what those once-trigger-happy-and-now-about-to-get-the-"Nova"-treatment Craydahls had done. And you know, a you-can-put-that-in-if-I-can-put-this-in compromise really did make sense, and the instant it received unanimous backing from us Brewsters, Marv started letting the air out of the dialogue pit. But, late as it was, we weren't done yet: Marv said nobody was going down for any R.E.M.-type z's until everybody's original choice—Jodi's Brent poster from her door, Dad's radioactive keepsake from the den mantel, Mom's homemade porch annoyance, and, of course, my raggedy old Raw Bar souvenir—had been tucked into the big bullet and buried in our backyard.

So we all split to ready our time-capsule items. Marv had recommended wrapping them individually in newspaper so that come 2001 it would feel as if we were opening

Christmas presents together. Plus, Marv thought it might be neat to read today's news thirteen years down the road.

While I was in my room wrapping my T-shirt in funny papers from the Sunday *Tribune*, it started to dawn on me what our state-assigned counselor was *really* up to. I mean, basically, we'd selected some of our touchiest items —these "special" things were really family sore points— and now Marv was getting us to bury them (Marv would say "preserve" them) for thirteen years! Well, I felt like I'd been had. I even started wrapping a substitute for my T-shirt, a faded old long-sleeved thing that had inspired the guys in my old dorm to call me Mr. Pajama Top. I ended up sticking with my T-shirt and Marv's game plan, though. Anything he was doing, I realized, he was only doing to help us Brewsters.

W E L L, we did it, thanks to our backyard floodlights and Marv's cheerleading. We took turns digging a four-foot-deep hole next to the family picnic table—the table had always served more as a bird-feeding station. Then we dropped the big bullet in, nose first. Marv had added the last item after we Brewsters had insisted that he contribute something. He'd balked, but then when he realized we were not kidding, he handed over his ballpoint—his initials were engraved on the clip—and in it went. It had become a nearly all-night counseling session, but the test of endurance was well worth it. At one point, while Mom was shoveling dirt back into the hole, I saw Dad put his arm around Jodi's waist. And later, while Dad was pounding an old croquet stake into the spot as a marker, Mom and Jodi surprised us guys by bringing French toast and pink champagne out to the picnic table. Soon I found myself kissing both gals on the cheek, and I don't think it was just the alcohol or maple syrup. By about three that morning, Marv told us that his work with us Brewsters was complete, and wished us good luck. He said he had to get up early the next morning, to ride with—and, I guess, counsel—a bickering car pool.

THINGS were unusually close in our family over the next few weeks. It was a shame we Brewsters weren't the ones getting the "Nova" treatment: They could have gotten some great footage of us gulping down dinner together again. We all still kept our plates on trays—you never know—but at least we parked these trays around the same table.

I even felt inspired enough to search the attic for the Brewster home movies—they'd been missing for years. I got quite a shock, though, after prying the lid off an old cookie canister: *Mom's time-capsule chimes were inside.* That really burned me, Mom evidently having played some shell game on the rest of us. So, that next Saturday, after Dad and Mom had packed sandwiches and driven off with Jodi to scout out some all-girl colleges, I decided to put Mom's chimes where they belonged.

There was a creepy, violating-the-tomb feeling to unearthing it, but the dirt was still so loose that I had the capsule out in about five minutes. And guess what I found in the newspaper around Mom's "chimes"? *A bunch of empty wooden sewing spools.* That got me so suspicious I tore away the want ads around Dad's little contribution. Inside was a wing nut all right, but this one was way smaller and *all* shiny. And then, Jodi's "Brent poster" turned out to be the location-of-Atlantis map I'd given her many Christ-mases before. I felt so darned naive to have actually wrapped my Raw Bar shirt. But I didn't rescue it. I re-wrapped everything, reburied the time capsule, and pounded the croquet stake back into the ground. Then I returned Mom's chimes to the cookie canister in the attic.

Of course I was disappointed, but there was no deny-ing that our whole family had warmed up considerably, and I'd have to have been a real jerk to raise any stink that might have disturbed all that. But I sure can't resist a little jab now and then. Like Dad and I will be watching some making-of-the-A-bomb docudrama on TV, and I'll say, "Dad—when we finally get your wing nut back out of the capsule, the Smithsonian's going to be offering you big bucks for it." And Dad will have to change the subject fast, or tell me to go ahead and put on whatever I want to watch—something that never happened *before* we buried our time capsule. And this morning, before leaving for work, I looked Mom right in the eye and told her that someone had just dumped half a ton of wooden spools on us at Trashmore, and did she need any *wooden spools*? She blushed and looked down at her shoes, and it made me wonder if, before New Year's Day, 2001, rolls around, I'll have been the only one to have dug down there and tampered with the Brewster Family Time Capsule.

After I Won
the Lottery

DRIVING back to work from the state lottery office in Milwaukee this afternoon, my second big check tucked safely behind the sun visor, I paid the thirty-five cents for a station wagon that was behind me at the Leech Lake toll booth. After I'd returned to freeway speed, the station wagon seemed kind of bashful—it looked like the driver was hanging back on purpose—so I eased my VW down to forty and held it there. I had a whole half-hour of lunch break left and a cheese-and-green-olive sandwich on my lap, so a leisurely drive back to the Christmas-tree farm where I work was okay by me. And eventually the station wagon I'd sponsored showed up alongside me. But instead of giving me any sign of thanks, the guy in the passenger's seat reached out and pelted my car with a handful of change. Then the station wagon shot off. With the last half of my sandwich trapped between my knees, I clung to the wheel, too freaked to do anything but hold my bug in its own lane. But as I began to mull over what had been happening to me ever since I'd won a million dollars in the lottery a year before, the money barrage didn't seem all that surprising.

A FEW mornings after I'd won the lottery, I stopped into the Satellite Diner with a gift I was sure would go over big. I'd always had a thing for Lanni, the dark-haired Hawaiian gal behind the counter, even though I knew she was seeing Al, the Satellite's owner. I caught her by the arm as she was clearing away the dishes from my breakfast special and fastened an expensive little watch around her wrist. "It isn't *really* for me," Lanni said, "is it?" I told her that it most certainly was. "Well, you shouldn't have!" she said, blushing as she looked it over. I told her it was nothing—that I'd just run into some luck recently—and pointed out the tiny Diamonel at the twelve o'clock position. She kept thanking me, and when Al got busy fishing something out of the deep fryer with a potato masher she snatched me a piece of lemon meringue pie. Later, when I got up to leave for work, she quickly leaned over the Formica and kissed me on the earlobe. I felt great, and I was still smiling that afternoon, underneath my surgical mask, while I sprayed white spruce with a needle fungicide.

The next morning, as I perched on my stool at the Satellite, Lanni ran over to take my order, even though she'd been in the middle of taking some other guy's order. And the morning after that, she gave me a complimentary orange juice in a milkshake glass, which I had to chug down before Al finished slipping new song titles into all the mini-jukeboxes at the booths. But as the days went by, Lanni seemed less and less excited to see me, and on the few occasions she did speak to me it was pretty awkward— more than it had ever been *before* I'd given her the watch, when she used to stop and chat with me about her glass-bird collection, or the last Louis L'Amour story she'd read, or the special tungsten heel her mom had to have put in. The whole thing made me feel a little like the man whose wife was gradually taken over by an unfriendly, alien life force in that "Twilight Zone" I'd seen so many times.

Finally, in a last-ditch effort to stay friends, I told Lanni there was an extra seat on the big Leech Lake fishing boat us guys from the Christmas-tree farm were chartering on the upcoming Saturday. She said she was already going river-tubing that day, and stressed the fact that it was with Al. Soon Lanni hardly ever waited on me. She always seemed to be involved in refilling something—salt shakers, pepper shakers, napkin dispensers, or already-full pancake-syrup pourers—about the time I rolled in for breakfast. So my order would get taken by the other counter lady, Carnella, a carrier of serious static charges due to her layers of shifting synthetic undergarments. Lanni did wait on me again—once, when Carnella was out sick—and really confused me with a sudden plate heaped with french fries after breakfast, while you-know-who was trying to unjam the toothpick dispenser next to the register. After eating a layer of fries off the top, though, I discovered a carefully folded napkin that contained the watch I'd given Lanni.

Well, I was determined not to make the same kind of mistake when Jerry's birthday arrived, a few months

later. Jerry is an old high-school buddy who works with
me at the Christmas-tree farm, and even though he was well
aware that my lottery win had turned everything affordable
on me, I didn't want any fancy price tag to come between
us. No, I simply decided to give Jerry the gift of literature.
See, I'm crazy about science fiction, especially the kind
where aliens from a dying planet crash-land on Earth, take
over human beings' bodies, worm their way into positions
of power, then warn Earthlings about the dangers of nuclear
experimentation, and—*poof*—disappear for good. Jerry
had always claimed he couldn't stand the stuff, but I refused
to believe he'd ever really given it a fair chance. Around
the farm he was always reading *Popular Mechanics* or one
of the manuals he kept in the bib pocket of his overalls,
like "How to"—I don't know—"Make Your Attic Livable,"
or "How to Turn Your Laundry Chute Into Storage Space."
Anyway, I bought Jerry a starter set of sci-fi classics, like
The Time Machine and *The War of the Worlds*—all on
tape from a Milwaukee outfit called Books-on-Cassette. I
loved picturing Jerry with his headset on, listening to, say,
Journey to the Center of the Earth while he tramped through
rows and rows of Douglas fir with his trimming knife. And
once he'd been turned on by the tapes he'd be free to start
borrowing from my extensive aliens-on-a-peace-mission
paperback collection. Anyway, I packed all twenty-six cassettes into the box my depth finder had come in, and gift-
wrapped it with a photocopy I'd bought of the actual front
page of the Milwaukee *Journal* from the day Jerry was born.
When I gave my present to Jerry, at work, a smile broke
out on his face that got wider as he turned the box over
in his hands and shook it. "Oh, boy—a cordless two-speed

drill, right?" he said, and he wasn't kidding. When he opened it, a letdown look replaced the smile. As he examined the cassettes, he said, "Well, I wouldn't have been able to guess it was this." Then he said, "You sure have inspired me to get my cassette player repaired." There was such an awkward silence that I just had to say something. I asked Jerry if I could borrow *Twenty Thousand Leagues Under the Sea*—it sort of popped out, unfortunately.

"Look, why don't you just take the whole works," Jerry said. He dropped the box on the ground and stalked off. I wished I was the Incredible Shrinking Man then, and could disappear down to about match-head size. Jerry steered clear of me for some months after that, teaming up to chain-saw trees at Thanksgiving with Howard Mason, the constant spitter, instead of with me.

Just before Christmas, I tried something else. I put a fifty into a special balsam-scented envelope and wrote on it, "To Buy Whatever You Want," and slid that into a plain envelope. I mailed the gift to Mona. I was sure she'd accept it. Mona, still technically my wife, had walked out on me two years earlier, and we'd spoken only once since: the morning after I won the lottery. I remembered waking up to her voice on the phone that day and thinking, Uh-oh. I'd used her full birth date for my six lucky lottery numbers. But all Mona wanted—at least then—was to say congratulations and tell me she'd seen the photo of me they ran in the newspaper and ask me when I'd started parting my hair on the other side. (I hadn't changed my part at all, which shows you how long two years of separation is.) Later—I'm still not sure why—I sent her an anonymous eighteen months of *Self* magazine. Well, the day after

Christmas Mona called to say hi and thank me for sending the cash.

I got real excited to find that someone might actually have accepted one of my gifts, and I asked her how she was going to spend it. She wasn't, she told me; on the advice of her lawyer, she had already mailed it back to me. We *were* still legally husband and wife, she reminded me, and said the lawyer had told her she would have a pretty strong claim if things got unfriendly. But going to court can be expensive and time-consuming, she said, and it would probably be a lot easier on both of us if I just began doing a few little things for her, like, for starters, sending her on an upcoming eclipse cruise. She said that according to the ad she'd cut out of the back of *Self*, you sailed the Indian Ocean diagonally, the whole time staying in the path of a total eclipse of the sun, so that it stayed dark for the better part of a day, while you got a candlelight brunch with unlimited champagne *and* a torchlight dinner while the scientists they had on board would explain what was actually going on and, later, maybe even ask you to the Captain's Ball, which would feature a Tahoe-style revue. Then they'd open up the twenty-four-hour casino for the remaining week, after which everyone would get a color memory album. Well, I figured I should do whatever was necessary to protect the bulk of my lottery winnings. So, dipping down into a reservoir of the same kind of strength that allows mothers to lift automobiles threatening the lives of their infants, I said to her, "Honey, start looking for a new set of luggage, because I'm putting you on that thing."

Mona is asking for stuff still, this summer. But fortunately it's been more like walkie-talkies, kayak lessons, and a watch, which, thanks to Lanni, I didn't have to go out of my way to get.

PULLING up this afternoon at the Pine River toll booth, the last one before my work exit, I started to give the attendant just my own thirty-five cents. I'd had it with trying to be generous. Then I noticed a knockout blonde in line behind me, wearing green sunglasses that matched her convertible, and I found myself pulling out another thirty-five cents. This time, once the tollgate lifted, I pushed the accelerator of my VW to the floor. It didn't do much good: in no time the convertible was there alongside me. But the blonde just raised her sunglasses and smiled at me. I tapped my horn once and gave her a don't-mention-it wave. Then she beeped back twice and raced off. I figured maybe I'd keep trying after all.

This Uncle

MY FRIEND Steve Riley, who lives in the only house in the neighborhood with a pool, gave his required five-minute presentation in speech class the other day. *Naturally*, it was all on his Uncle Jack and, of course, lasted more like ten minutes. Steve's number one topic since the day he moved onto our block has been his Uncle Jack.

Steve began his Uncle Jack speech by yanking an old tablecloth off an unoccupied desk in the front row. Sitting there was the petrified skull of a baby dinosaur. (Normally it's hanging from the ceiling over Steve's bed on eighty-pound test line.) The story goes that his Uncle Jack discovered it while galloping full-tilt across a desert to warn some prospectors about a sandstorm. Later in his speech, Steve got to my favorite Uncle Jack story, this one about the greyhound his uncle got as a reward for accidentally interrupting a robbery at a racetrack. I always like the part about how whenever Uncle Jack's phone rings, the dog automatically gets into the ready-to-race position. After his speech (he concluded that he was lucky to have such an amazing uncle), Steve got applause the whole way back to his desk, something that seldom happens in the eighth grade.

I actually met Uncle Jack once, the same summer he showed up at the Rileys with the dinosaur skull for Steve. He had a permanent outdoor squint, like Roy Rogers, and a deep tan and some scars across one cheek; it looked as if a cat—a *big* cat—had swiped at him. (Steve told me later that the scars came from riding smack into the arm of some rare and poisonous cactus, and that the accident had laid him out with a fever of a hundred and four.) I remember Uncle Jack giving me and Steve packs of fire-crackers—the brand name was Rhino Chasers—on the condition we wouldn't tell anyone where they came from. "Even if you lose fingers," he said, which only upped the excitement. A few days after Uncle Jack left, Steve asked me if I had checked out his uncle's black leather money belt, something he had brought up plenty of times before— and he got really pissed when I said I hadn't noticed it. (I *had*, though.)

A L L I'd ever had, uncle-wise, was this old Uncle Cameron, from a place called Lumberville, and he died in his sleep awhile back from what Dad, his younger brother, called "complications from diabetes." He wasn't an uncle you'd particularly want to stand up and give a speech on. Except for his being born with an extra little toe on each foot, there weren't many great Uncle Cameron stories to tell.

Not unless you wanted to go into his daily ritual of injecting himself with insulin, or felt like holding up, as some kind of visual aid, his triple-E-width slippers, which still live in the back of our guest-room closet.

Uncle Cameron looked a lot like the fat guy in Laurel and Hardy, and usually wore these really cheap gray elastic suspenders. He was forever cleaning out the same dirty pipe while he bragged about all the medical things he'd been through, like root canal. Whenever Uncle Cameron visited us, he'd bring along another brick of fruitcake, which seemed heavier every time. For himself, he'd have a bag of his own little sugar-free cookies— plain-looking things with a hole in the middle. He'd stick them on the end of his finger and munch away till he broke through to the hole, when it would all fall into his lap or onto the floor. He had a funny smell, which I had imagined came from all the artificial sweeteners logjammed in his system until Dad told me it was from the epoxies Uncle Cameron came into daily contact with in his vinyl-repair business. His favorite phrase was "everybody and his brother," and way too many of Uncle Cameron's stories boiled down to how everybody and his brother had butted in ahead of him on some investment deal and made off with a real bundle. One story I actually did think was neat was about the time Uncle Cameron took what he swore was half his life savings and invested it in a concrete dinosaur park. (That's the only Uncle Cameron story I ever told Steve.) But then, wouldn't you know, everybody and his brother had panicked and bailed out of this prehistoric park at the very last second, leaving Uncle Cameron to lose his shirt.

So, anyway, that was Uncle Cameron, and that's

partly why dinner the other night turned into such a surprise. Because right after I'd raved to my folks about how great Steve's speech on his Uncle Jack had been, and then grumbled some about Uncle Cameron, Dad hit me with some *really* weird uncle news: Turns out, see, that this coming Sunday, Easter, we're getting visited by some *new* uncle, this Uncle Al, who I never even knew existed. Dad said he's just his and Uncle Cameron's little step-brother, and that I met him once when I was too young to remember it. My folks said they hadn't heard from him in years, until they got a postcard from him last Christmas saying he'd gotten divorced and had returned to the bachelor life. He'd moved from California to just a little ways west of us and was living above a hobby store he'd bought called the Coin Den. None of that made him sound too promising; I mean, he sounded miles away from Steve's Uncle Jack.

SOMETIMES I like to make up all these amazing uncle stories that I might be able to tell people if *I* had some kind of Uncle Jack for an uncle. Like maybe there'd be one about how after this uncle of mine had stopped a holdup at some diner down South, they'd awarded him free pan-cakes for life, so that anytime he dropped by the diner— even if it was to use the pay phone—they'd make him sit down and have a stack of buttermilks, on the house. Or there might be another story Dad would have told me about how when this uncle of mine had been handling snakes in a carnival, he'd had to give himself daily injec-tions of snake venom, so that whenever he got bit by one of the cobras his resistance would be so built up that he'd get a fever of something like a hundred and six but wouldn't die. And every time this uncle would visit us, I can see him bringing me some really neat item, too. Like a jar of moose meat, say, or some strange rock that had crashed through the roof of a pool hall and landed a cue stick away from where he'd been standing—not showing up with some old concrete fruitcake. And during his stay, I'd catch a glimpse of the rodeo scars that Mom would have already told me covered 25 percent of his body and were better left unmentioned. And when my folks weren't around, maybe he'd show me how to flip a cigarette up and catch it in the corner of my mouth, so the next morning I could go down the block and teach it to Steve Riley. And then Steve would call later, and this wild uncle of mine would be invited to use Steve's backyard pool, too, and right off he'd do a really choice cannonball off the board that would get all the Rileys absolutely soaked, and I'd be feeling so proud when he climbed out of the water, those rodeo scars over 25 percent of his body.

W E L L, this what you could call "lost" uncle—Uncle Al of the Coin Den—drove up on Sunday in time for our big Easter lunch. He was just this medium-sized guy in a short-sleeved white shirt with a swordfish stitched into the pocket. He had red hair pushed straight back like he was facing into serious wind, and he had wrinkles around his eyes that were most likely from squinting at dates on old pennies. The only real scars I could see on him were left over from zits. Maybe I didn't expect to see anything as neat as a money belt, but I did expect to see *something.* This Uncle Al wore no belt, and his golf slacks hung kind of low on his hips.

Anyway, he was pretty shy at first, not saying much. I started thinking, Uh-oh. But then he came right out with a pretty decent prayer before the meal that went like this: "Good bread, good meat—Good God, let's eat!" That one could definitely get you a laugh in speech class.

While my folks were busy dishing out Mom's Beef Fantasia, Uncle Al caught my eye, tossed a grape in the air, and caught it in his mouth. It was weird: I liked it, but I felt embarrassed, too—I guess because he seemed to be doing it just for me. Eventually, of course, Dad got around to complaining to Uncle Al about how slow everything's been in the driver's training business. Dad said that if things didn't pick up soon, he wouldn't be able to afford to have any more dual-braking systems put into the learners. Uncle Al chewed and thought for a while. Then he told Dad that as long as he had students driving all around anyway, he ought to get some kind of taxi biz going at the same time. Boy, did Dad ever like that! He immediately started doing a lot of math on both sides of his napkin. And as Mom scraped and stacked the plates, she started apologizing to Uncle Al for how tired she said she must look, hinting that it was all due to Dad's snoring. Uncle Al leaned back in his chair till it touched the wall behind him and swung his legs. Then he suggested that Mom sew a pocket into the back of Dad's pajama top and drop in a tennis ball every night before bed. This would keep Dad from sleeping on his back and, as a result, keep him from snoring. Mom thought that that was plain brilliant and left for her sewing machine.

This Uncle

With our Easter meal basically over and my folks both so preoccupied, Uncle Al asked me if I wanted to take a spin. His car's roof, which I took to be vinyl when he first pulled up, turned out to be a convertible top. And soon, while we're cruising around town, top down, Uncle Al says, "What this," and he taps his horn as we pass a yard sale and waves like everyone there knows him, and, do you know, everyone there waves right back at us like they do, which was embarrassing but cracked me up anyway.

Later—it's while we're sitting in a booth at a drive-in and having root beer floats—Uncle Al starts teaching me this game he invented called It's Possible. You play it by making up things that are entirely possible about strangers who pass by. You can't make up just *anything*, though. It has to be a *possible* connection that might exist between a stranger and you. So like when a kid my age walked by our booth swinging a bag from the Jeans Barn, Uncle Al said he got a wrong number a few days back, some kid asking for "Rory"—and he said how it's possible, wasn't it, that this was the very kid who called. "Or else," he added, "maybe *that's* Rory." Well, I didn't know what to say for my turn. Eventually, I came up with how it was possible that the kid had just had a hamburger from the very same steer as the meat in Mom's Beef Fantasia, which I guess was passable for a first-time player. But then I told Uncle Al that inside the kid's shopping bag was the same exact pair of jeans I'd tried on at the Jeans Barn last week but didn't buy because they made me look stupid. And Uncle Al really laughed at that, which made me feel great.

Soon, while driving up Center Street, we came across a swarm of high-school kids in band uniforms, and drummers warming up in a big way alongside a papier-mâché

Egyptian barge that didn't have any connection to Easter *I* could see. For a good five blocks ahead, both sides of the street are packed with people, lots of them in church clothes and fancy bonnets, standing maybe four deep, and that's not counting the kids all over the curb. And there's a cop with white gloves blocking Center Street, gesturing for us to turn right onto Hawthorn.

"No problem, chief," Uncle Al says to him, slowing to a halt, while at the same time cranking up the baseball game he's had on at low volume the whole time. "Darn ball game always fades out on me when I cross town any other way," he yells to the cop over what's now blaring play-by-play. Then he adds, "But so be it," like, "That's life" and "It's certainly not your fault," and he salutes the cop a good one.

"Well," the cop says, "I guess there's still time." And soon we're cruising down the middle of the parade route. And shy Uncle Al starts smiling and waving and honking at the crowd lining the street, and even though everyone knows we're certainly not the parade, Uncle Al's acting like we are, and people seem to find that funny and join in on the act and wave back and whistle. Then Uncle Al gets up and sits on top of his seat and steers with his feet, letting the car's drive gear just roll us down Center Street. So then I move up, too, and I wave and I feel good about myself in some dumb way and real good about my new Uncle Al, who's going to be generating some pretty unusual sorts of uncle stories, which you can bet Steve Riley will be hearing very soon.

37 Years

T H I S is never very easy," Dr. Tudor said. "But it showed up, plain as day, after your physical. It's going to be quite a shock—you, a healthy young man of thirty-seven and all—but it's my job to level with you. Believe me, now's when I wish I was testing seat belts or something. Because you have exactly thirty-seven years left to live."

I'd had a feeling it wasn't going to be good news, but . . . cut down in thirty-seven more years . . . it was almost too much. My mind went numb, and I searched Dr. Tudor's face for some small ray of hope. But all he said was "Go ahead and scream if you want. I wouldn't blame you."

Scream? I couldn't even make my mouth say bye-bye. I just wandered out of Dr. Tudor's office, and—maybe ten minutes later, maybe two hours later—found myself wading barefoot through the reflecting pool in front of the library. Nickels, dimes, even pennies felt good under my feet and between my toes. I tried to feel which presidents were on them. Then some guy, all silver buttons, shouted at me to get out, but he needn't have wasted his energy: I'd decided to get out anyway, before I got any sadder. See, I loved the feeling of being barefoot. But how many more times would I be able to squeeze going barefoot into the final thirty-seven years of my life?

I had more hard questions for myself during the long drive home. Like why hadn't I ever slept in a lighthouse before? And how come my years of collecting metal cigar tubes seemed so foolish now? And why hadn't I just gone ahead and tramped something like "Bring Me the Head of Ronald McDonald" into the snow on the hill next to the exit ramp, instead of only *thinking* about doing it? Or pulled up the carpeting in the living room to see what's been causing the little lump that's in the middle every day and in front of the fireplace every night? And why hadn't I ever bothered to get HIYA put on my rear license plate? Just who did I think I was kidding with the way I'd been "living"?

Well, when I finally walked in the door that evening, I didn't say a word about my visit to Dr. Tudor. Can you imagine—"Hey, honey! Kids! Take a good look at me during 'Entertainment Tonight' and dinner because in thirty-seven years . . ." No way. I was crazy about my wife, Valinda, our daughter, Jenny, and Liza, the little neighbor girl who was around so much she was all ours except for the paperwork. And I didn't think that *they* should have to carry around any of this new weight inside me. But, you know, I guess I misjudged just how heavy that weight really was. Because after I'd lied to them, told them things were awfully slow now in the pool-table-sales game and that I'd be home barefoot a lot over the next year, that heaviness dragged me right down to the basement bar. I never even bothered to flick on the beer sign down there. Just stretched out on one of the pool tables in the dark, drinking whiskey straight out of a bottle through a flexible straw to try to dissolve the lead bowling ball buried deep in my stomach. Yeah, and at first that was good medicine. But then later, after two straight weeks of the police bringing me home just as it was getting light, and with my memory so loused up that, no, I honestly *didn't* remember sleeping in the shallow end of the penguin pool or in the tulips growing along the floral clock's big hand . . . well, that just had to be rough on my Valinda, and on my Jenny, and on our neighbors' little Liza.

So if I didn't want to keep hurting them or go handing in my room key thirty-seven years early on an already tight schedule, I had to clean up my act while there was still time. First I turned the caps on all the liquor bottles in the house just as tight as they'd go. Then I rounded up Valinda and Jenny and Liza, herded them into the laundry room, and told them the truth.

Geez, I'd underestimated them! They were so strong they just stood or sat on the machines and watched me while I cried. And right away some of the heaviness of that weight that was lodged in my gut lifted. We'd always been close, but now, it seemed to me, we drew even closer. Those three gals of mine became my pillars of strength, and when they really couldn't be home with me, they'd leave notes like "Honey—Margo still wants to try cutting and frosting my hair. Back soon," or "Daddy—Me and

Liza are walking to the mall to buy rabbits. See you in time for dinner. Love, Jenny."

Boy, just tell a guy he's got only thirty-seven years left on the planet and, once he's finished going a few rounds with the whiskey bottle, watch him scramble for meaning. Watch him turn off "Mary Tyler Moore" reruns he's seen three times and, instead, get outside and enjoy life, maybe drive to the bank, maybe take the long way. Watch him gradually cut his sleep time from eight hours to, say, seven and a quarter. Then see him decide there'll be no more reading Stephen King's *Cujo* and then going to the movie *Cujo* two months later. See him start picking one or the other—no more of this "both" stuff.

What Dr. Tudor probably doesn't know is that he's actually done me a favor. Sure, I "got through" those first thirty-seven years, but now I'm going to start making every day of the next thirty-seven really count. You want to know something else? Back when I was living like some immortal fool, my life was never very exciting. But *now*—heck, I get a big charge out of just taking a key down to the hardware store and watching them make a duplicate. *I might not even need it.* But the sight of all those different-colored keys hanging on their hooks, and . . . ummmm . . . the manly smell of ground metal—those are experiences you can't go on having forever. Because that's another thing: I used to *smell,* right? But now, thanks to Dr. Tudor, my senses are turned up so crazy high, I'm *smell-ING.* And where I used to *see,* now I'm *see-ING.* For instance, for thirty-seven years a pink pocket comb lying on the sidewalk was just a pink pocket comb lying on the sidewalk. But now—*now*—it's suddenly a five-inch-long bubble-gum-colored pink pocket comb with twenty-three thick teeth and thirty-three thin ones and BOBBIE'S HAIR SHACK in gold stamped on the spine and UNBREAKABLE in raised pink letters next to it, lying on the sidewalk near a newsstand, three feet away from a ripped-off cover of *Bear Archery Digest*. See what I mean? Sure, I may have only thirty-seven years left until I sign off, but at least we're talking, I think, about thirty-seven years of some kind of heightened reality. And someday, soon, I might even do some parachuting off observation decks.

Getting Herbert Back

W HILE it may be as dry as dust around the rest of the state, here in Crescent Valley it's been raining and raining and then raining some more. So that all the kidding about arks that you'd hear at the beginning, when there was only minor flooding, has mostly vanished since Highway 82 washed away in big chunks of asphalt and the voices came booming down from helicopters, saying to boil all drinking water. What also vanished as the water rose, and then rose again even more, was most of the optimism Crescent City had prided itself on. Some residents already sound defeated now when they tell you it's been raining for twelve days straight, while other folks, getting all whiny about it, will swear it's been at least fourteen. But today, the stubbornly optimistic head of our now disbanded sandbagging brigade, Malone, eased a soggy bank calendar out of his wallet to try and prove to me it's been what he called "a mere ten days." It just seems like more to the rest of us.

Actually, we Crescent Valley residents who haven't yet evacuated are becoming less and less concerned with exactly how long it's been raining. We're more likely now to start out talking number of sandbags. I mean, even though things are way beyond sandbags, we can't help doing some Monday-morning quarterbacking about the number of sandbags and the thickness and height of the walls of sandbags that started out keeping the floodwaters of the Mouse River from our homes, but after a while didn't. All of which usually leads us into talking about the damage. Talking about the damage is mainly what we do, unless we actually venture out and make ourselves inspect the damage. I did that to myself again recently. Just the other day, I said to hell with the swollen-joint pain I still feel from heaving sandbags, and I set out through the downpour in my duck boat. I oared high over my fields, easily clearing the top of the fence separating my un-insured corn crop from the road. And an hour later, when I was back home rubbing a hot liniment into my elbows and staring out the window of my dear departed Effie's (lightning took her last year) second-story sewing room, where I'm holed up now, I witnessed even more damage. My Ford truck, followed by a half-dozen duck decoys from the garage, floated out over the front yard, do-si-doed around what was still showing of the evergreen, then got caught by a strong surge of Mouse River spillover that swept it clear across to where, at least in my mind, Effie's garden still sits. Until finally, those bobbing decoys got caught in a tangle of telephone wires and poles that had already snagged a drowned steer and a propane tank from a camper.

Rowing over to any farm or home in Crescent Valley where folks still live can't help but give you a sense of people expecting the worst. My latest social outing was to the Byquists', yesterday, and it was strenuous oaring with numb arms for what wasn't a particularly fun time. The entire day, in fact, was spent preparing the Byquists' second story for the worst. Their ground floor was underwater— the Byquists are on pretty low ground—and their upstairs already had an inch of water and a strong wet-dog odor. Ralph Byquist, Crescent Valley's fire chief, was pulling out the bottom couple of drawers from each upstairs desk and dresser and stacking them up on top. Louise Byquist, who isn't half as perky as she was before Highway 82 washed out, was in charge of all the upstairs draperies. She sloshed around in a pair of Ralph's firemen's boots, her mouth full of pins (that reminded me of my Effie), and she hemmed up all the floor-length draperies exactly two feet. Raising everything two feet was Ralph's upstairs strategy.

While I stacked red bricks for the Byquists' furniture to stand on, I tried cheering up Ralph and Louise by making believe I'd been happy to see my crummy old truck with over a hundred thou on it get swept away. But Louise just kept tripping into the water, and Ralph complained I'd raised his recliner only twenty inches, and then he dropped a floor-length mirror he'd been trying to nail up higher, which broke on a stack of bricks. Louise nearly swallowed her pins. I just stood there, feeling what I'm sure the Byquists must have felt: raising everything around you like that only made you smaller and smaller in a predicament that already had you feeling pretty teeny and powerless. Then Ralph slipped while attempting to make the stretch from a step stool to his recliner, barely missing Louise.

After raising all we could, we perched on kitchen stools rescued earlier from downstairs. The raindrops sounded like marbles hitting the roof. Finally, after polishing off a few warm cans of beer salvaged by Ralph, we talked about all anyone remaining in Crescent Valley talks about once they're tired of talking about the damage: Herbert.

We stickers—we Crescent Valley residents who haven't yet evacuated—are hoping that getting Herbert back to Crescent Valley will make a difference. And none of us are especially superstitious or put much stock in astrology or UFO sightings or the stupid fortune-cookie predictions made by Janadu, the talking robot from last summer's traveling carnival. But getting Herbert back makes more and more sense as a remedy for our rain. And if you want to know the truth, we're depending on it working.

JIM KNOX, a Crescent Valley plumber, volunteered to bring Herbert back. He raised his hand during an emergency meeting we stickers held at the Kozy Kettle Restaurant, right after our first full week of nonstop rain, and immediately after a National Weather Service observer became the first victim of our flooding. (He'd swum to an elm tree after his canoe flipped over in a crosscurrent.

That tree, though, was also the high ground picked by dozens of panicked snakes.) The news of his bad luck convinced the majority of Crescent Valley folks to evacuate, with, of course, the help of the Red Cross. Everyone came to the emergency meeting in hip boots or trout waders. We voted to double Jim Knox's weekly plumbing take while he did the finding. Downright generous, too, considering the drop in demand for local plumbing work. Anyway, Jim Knox left to track down Herbert and to try and bring him back to Crescent Valley pronto.

Jim was already experienced in trying to locate a person. Years ago, his teenage daughter, Pam, ran off heading west, hoping to get into some fancy cooking school out there—or so the story goes. But Jim never found her. And, supposedly, Jim's own special brand of not-so-funny humor was one of the things that drove her off. (After she'd been gone a week, I remember Jim barging into a conversation that I was having with Bob Clark, the train engineer, to tell me for the nth time how Pam's room was just how she had left it. "Her bed *still* isn't made," he'd laughed, "so when she's had it with garlic and everything, she can come back and make it.") Those of us sticking it out in Crescent Valley now would have a much easier time enjoying Jim's brand of humor *if* Jim showed up back here with Herbert.

EVERYBODY in Crescent Valley knows Herbert, because of the way Herbert got around town. Wearing his deerskin jacket with the fringe, his arms motionless at his sides, he'd generally walk from the Shell station to the farm co-op to the bank. Then, after touching the bank, he'd go to the Kozy Kettle to the First Presbyterian to the firehouse. And then from the firehouse to the railroad station to the grain elevator. And then, finally, over to the school in time to watch them jump rope. (Herbert didn't jump rope himself; he just seemed to like to watch.) And when recess was over he'd turn around and retrace his whole route.

We used to think Herbert was just a simpleton—someone who's most likely plus or minus a chromosome and who sleeps in leaning barns. Then we started to find out that Herbert and the term "simpleton" don't even belong in the same furrow together. For one thing, he started finding items that had been lost. Sometimes that only meant buttons. But Herbert also located an envelope containing a land deed that the bank had long since given up on ever finding. And then he located five cows belonging to Arch Weber that had wandered off in fog to southern marshland. The fast talker from last summer's traveling carnival called him a "boy with special sense." But Herbert wasn't convinced by the guy to join up with his show.

THERE'S been word from Jim Knox, on a motel postcard. And the joker wrote his message backwards. He didn't have any great news; I mean, he hadn't located Herbert yet. But he didn't think he was too far off Herbert's path, and his joke about the "erutsiom" (moisture) back here in Crescent Valley was—well, it was almost reassuring that Jim Knox hadn't lost his own special brand of humor. Unfortunately, it's especially hard to enjoy Jim's humor right now. But at least it's a sign that in spite of all of Jim's lonesome driving and searching and motel staying, he's still himself. Go, Jim.

M A L O N E roared over today in his amazing powerboat that leaves a huge wake. All of us stickers have been eyeing that boat and that wake with increasing envy. I'm sure deep down, though, it's Malone's all-the-time optimism about our situation that we're really envying. Malone, who owns the Kozy Kettle Restaurant and who directed our long-ago disbanded sandbagging brigade, was still looking on the bright side after the failure of our sandbags. "All our backs could use a break anyway," he'd say. "And look," he liked to add, "we all finally have the lakefront homes we've been dreaming of."

Malone tied his machine next to my duck boat. Then he dove through the window of my dear Effie's upstairs sewing room, and onto the couch I sleep on. He was wearing his bright yellow rain poncho. I made coffee over Sterno I'd rescued from my downstairs, and we talked. Malone had just received a mail drop on the red roof of his Kozy Kettle establishment. He said that seeing the parachute open had taken him back to "the good ol' days in the Pacific theater." He seemed happy, getting to play PT boat again while delivering what little mail there is to what few people are left. But then, of course, I don't remember ever seeing him unhappy.

He had news from Jim Knox. It was a postcard of the Route #5 Coach House, someplace out West. Jim hadn't located "trebreH" (Herbert) yet. But he *had* talked to people who'd supposedly talked to people who'd supposedly seen Herbert. And he'd met a jogger who said that a hitchhiker in a deerskin jacket had found a stopwatch he'd lost in tall weeds just off the road. In his signoff, Jim Knox even attempted a joke about collecting Crescent Valley rainwater in canning jars and selling it out of town. Keep a-going, Jim.

Before Malone sped off to deliver the rest of the mail, I had to tell him about the water currently seeping into the town's grain elevator and creeping up between the kernels of corn. Malone says that when all this is over I should insist that it's *my* corn up there at the very top, which to me sounded like a borderline Jim Knox comment. However, talking about things like the flood damage and Jim Knox's progress in looking for Herbert beats sitting on your hands and listening to the steady din of half-an-inch-in-diameter raindrops—on roofs, against windows, over the water—that there's no getting away from. Even cupping your hands over your ears isn't an escape: sure, you can shut out the rain, but you get just as steady a hum in the space where the sound of the rain has been for so long.

TONIGHT, Mitchell, who runs the Shell station, showed up outside my sewing room window in his inflatable fisherman's dinghy. He was out checking out the damage. He told me that back before our phone went dead, he called his mom in Deacon City, only forty-eight miles north of us. And Mitchell said she had a hard time believing our situation here, what with Deacon City corn standing tinder dry and new Deacon City laws against washing cars and tractors. Well, that only made us stickers feel more and more alone in a predicament that already had us feeling plenty lonely. And as our downpour continues, it's giving us stickers a new kind of feeling altogether: the vague feeling that we've done something wrong. An extreme form of that showed its colors recently, when a few of us managed to rescue Bob Clark, the engineer, from a gradually sinking Dodge. Inside we found Bob Clark, unconcious. Then we found the rope around Bob Clark's legs that Bob Clark himself must have tied. And when he came to, he was muttering about Herbert. See, we all felt bad when Herbert left—or when we *made Herbert leave,* which would be more accurate. Bob Clark was the main one insisting that Crescent Valley would be better off without Herbert. And none of the rest of us disagreed.

HERBERT'S talent at finding lost objects—what the carnival man labeled his "special sense"—helped Herbert to get by. Finding some keys missing from Malone's Kozy Kettle, for example, earned him a week of pancake breakfasts. And recovering two hard-to-locate hubcaps was good for lunch money from Mitchell's Shell Station. And while we're not a town of real losers here, we were misplacing enough stuff to keep Herbert going.

Then Herbert started having this streak of above-average days, followed right away by these really amazing days when he'd find lots and lots of lost items on his walk around town. Too many items, really, because more and more frequently Herbert was finding items that people never wanted found—things that were never meant to be found and that only disturbed people when they were.

Like, for example, the Polaroids from our farm co-op's last New Year's Eve bash that Herbert recovered from a ditch, which made Miss Rexella Johns, a fifth-grade teacher, move first to Deacon City, and then, we heard, to Webster Lake.

As Herbert found more of these disturbing items, his rewards slowed and then stopped coming altogether. No longer was any lost item ever rewarded with a meal or with change. And that's when the real trouble began; that's when Herbert started telling people around town what was going to happen before it did. For instance, he told me he was sorry about Effie. Only this was two days before she'd tried to get all the clothes off the line when that thunderstorm struck. In all truth, Herbert's crystal-ball ability wasn't so bad when he could tell Mrs. Olar that she was going to have twin boys, and I know Stew Parker was mostly pleased to find out ahead that he held the winning ticket for the school raffle. But it was hard to take when Herbert predicted the bad things: it was too much like it was his fault somehow, although logically I knew darned well that he didn't make the lightning hit Effie. So later, when Herbert told Ben Buchanan about Ben's incurable illness, and Ben jumped in front of the eight-forty express from Webster Lake, we decided to kick Herbert out of Crescent Valley for good. (Of course, he already had a knapsack packed.)

The rain started a few days later. And, granted, it was pretty close to the time the cloud-seeding experiments began over Clinton Valley way, and around the time the atmosphere was suddenly supposed to be loaded with bits of volcanic ash. So it is possible that Herbert's departure is just some straw we've been grabbing at; maybe we've been fooling ourselves all along.

I'M TOLD that Ralph and Louise Byquist's strategy of raising everything in their upstairs two feet has been replaced by a new strategy: trying to ignore all the spiders as they make do in their attic on only small amounts of food from their shrinking stock. I'm also doing my best to cope, but my elbows are getting too achey to make more trips in my duck boat. I'm fortunate to have on hand still some canned pears, packs of beef jerky, and a dry Perry Mason mystery. I'm having more and more trouble sleeping, however, and what sleep I do get is so light and dreamy. In a recent dream, I was kayaking painlessly around town atop my old Ford truck. All that was left above the lake covering Crescent Valley was the top of the First Presbyterian's bell tower. It clanged like a buoy as I passed.

MALONE came by again today, and I'm honestly starting to hate that fancy powerboat of his, even if it does bring news. Malone is still looking on the bright side, and to hear him talk about how this year's corn prices weren't so hot anyway, you'd think that we farmers were actually going to have topsoil for next year's corn.

Malone did have more news from Jim Knox. Jim wrote that descriptions of Herbert are now posted in zillions of grocery stores out West. But he also said that he's beginning to think that the only person who could find Herbert would probably be Herbert himself. What have I said about Jim's own special brand of not-so-funny humor? Anyway, Jim said he's getting tired of motels every night, and that his last stay at one turned into a real-life bad dream, something we stickers can sure sympathize with. Seems he woke up in the morning to find that most of the other motel guests had faces wrapped like mummies. Well, turns out he'd registered too late the night before to notice the clinic for plastic surgery across the street. And it was funny, picturing Jim caught in that situation—remember, this is the same guy who was still kidding about arks after the Mouse River had claimed Highway 82. But maybe it only seemed funny because nothing else has made us stickers laugh much lately.

MITCHELL was by again in his dinghy. Says that the awful shrieks and screams coming out of an abandoned farmhouse near his Shell station turned out to be a pair of bobcats, crouching terrified in the attic where they'd taken refuge. That was the kind of news I probably didn't need to hear. On the lighter side, Mitchell reports that fish are jumping in the vicinity of the bank, and that, on his way over, he paddled by two partially submerged cars, drifting along with their headlights on. Something to do with the water completing the circuit, Mitchell told me.

ANOTHER postcard from Jim Knox, and for crying out loud, what are we supposed to do now? Jim has learned that Herbert is touring the West with the same traveling carnival that came through Crescent Valley last summer. Herbert is evidently performing in place of Janadu, the talking robot who was making all those vague kind of predictions. But Jim also said that he's abandoning Herbert's trail—"temporarily," he said—so he can try and find the gal whose photo and daily recipe column appear in some local newspaper he's come across. "She has all Pam's features," he wrote; at least that's how it reads forwards. He seems convinced that this is *his* Pam, the daughter-fled-to-cooking-school he failed to find years back. It's a fatherly enough quest and all, but where does that leave us stickers?

The very highest places in Crescent Valley, the places higher than our own rooftops, still haven't been properly safety-checked. According to Malone, the low ground where the Byquists lived is now one big lake, with only poor Ralph and Louise's rooftop antenna breaking the surface. Malone is positive they made it to higher ground, but I'm not so sure.

Evacuating by small boat has become near impossible, what with all the tricky new currents in our steadily rising water. Sure, Malone and some of us stickers selected by fair coin tosses could probably make it out of Crescent Valley squeezed into his powerful rig. But Malone doesn't believe that'll be necessary, and his all-the-time optimism is going to keep him here no matter what. So what am I supposed to do? The water now covers my upstairs baseboards. So what do I do now if I don't want to end up treading water? Continue waiting for Jim Knox to show up someday with Herbert? Or stabilize my duck boat with the eight empty bleach bottles I've collected?

Mom and Pop Biz

BACK about the beginning of summer, I started feeling guilty because I hadn't written my folks in a while. So I called them long distance, and boy, did they have some big news: They'd finally sold their tiny live-bait shop after all these years and retired. So of course I congratulated them, but then, as the conversation started to wind down . . . well, I don't know. I must have sounded a little too complainy about my free-lance writing career or something, because a week later I got a letter from Mom and Dad on their old live-bait-shop stationery saying that they were going to start up their own magazine. And they were practically begging me to send them some of my stuff.

Now, it sounded like it was just going to be some kind of little mom-and-pop magazine, really, but damn, were they excited about it in their letter. "Son, we're interested in anything and everything," Mom wrote, and at the bottom of the letter Dad added, "Your mother's and my only requirement, fella, is that the material be good. Remember, it would probably be a mistake to try and tailor a piece specifically for us."

Right off the bat, though, I totally ignored Dad's advice. Really, because if my first submission to them—an article I titled "Retired? Sure—But Busier Than All Get Out"—had been any *more* tailored for them, I might as well have attached cleaning instructions. So I guess I shouldn't have been so surprised to get it right back.

"I'm sure you didn't *mean* it to be so obvious" was all Mom wrote. And Dad—hell, I could hardly believe that this was the same guy who used to throw lawn darts with me those summer evenings until way after sundown.

"I'm afraid I more than agree with your mother on this one," he wrote. " 'Obvious,' she says? Well, no kidding! But also really tailored. And what did I just get done telling you, last letter? Plus the whole I'm-retired-but-look-how-busy-I-am angle of your article . . . Mother in Heaven! Didn't you feel like you were dangling your worm in some pretty heavily fished waters when you wrote it? Sorry, but it gets a great big NO from me. Chin up, though, fella. Margie"—my sister—"who, incidentally, just officially untied the knot with that river guide, Norv, and is staying in your old room here until she gets her court reporting back up to speed, claims she 'found things in it to admire all the way through.' I only wish your mother and I had, too. By the way, next time round, don't forget to enclose return postage."

Well, I took this rejection pretty hard. I mean, it was a lot more intense than, say, *Argosy* rejecting me. But, you know, after sleeping for two days and thirteen hours, I woke up with everything back in perspective. Sure, Mom and Dad had conceived me, fed me, and taught me how to tease a largemouth bass with an injured minnow. But that didn't mean when I'd grown up they were automatically going to love every single thing that came out of my typewriter. After all, it wasn't like every single finger painting I'd ever brought home from kindergarten got taped to the side of the reserve frog tank in my folks' basement, either.

So I threw myself headlong into a new article I eventually titled "The Divorce Experience: Mixer-Upper or Putter-Back-Togetherer?" This one landed in the psychological/inspirational category, and I was positive Mom and Dad would really go for it. I was so anxious waiting for their reactions, though, that I volunteered for jury duty, just as a distraction. But after being sequestered in a Howard Johnson's every night for three weeks and losing $97.54 at poker *and* gaining something in the neighborhood of twenty pounds, I'd had enough. I accidentally-on-purpose looked at our guard's newspaper to disqualify myself, sped home in a cab, and ripped open the bait-shop envelope sitting in my mailbox.

Mom wrote, "It's a one-idea piece, but it's such an interesting idea, and what with your painstaking attention to the various psychological complications of divorce . . . well, Son, I think it's a real find." Good ol' Mom. Even the old man came through: "Not you at the top of your form, certainly, and the business where the make-believe divorced daughter in your example runs off to join the B-12 worshipers in Oregon should probably be saved for the ending or, better yet, cut out completely. But with some careful editing . . . why not?"

But then Margie, the sister I'd never even yelled at

the time she lost my good pair of red-dice cuff links at a dance, had to chime in with her opinion. She wrote, "It never, not even for a second, worked for me. Predictable and mean-spirited, and it squeezes the daylights out of small events in the experiences of divorcées for no apparent reason."

And then—I could hardly believe my eyes—Uncle Foster, that old coot, who, for my birthdays, used to send me IOUs on the back of old jai alai betting stubs, had to get in on the act, too. "I'm just camping out here with your folks until the weather gets warmer and we've got the first issue of the magazine off the ground," he wrote. "But as far as your article goes, I must say, the watch-your-back-divorcée-coming-through attitude throughout the thing seems awfully, awfully familiar nowadays, and your parents, after hearing me and your sister out on your article, have swung around to our side. But if it lifts your spirits any, we also agreed that you can do much better."

Depressed? Yeah, and I had a right to be. It just didn't seem fair. But my folks hadn't raised a quitter. I kept thinking, I'll show 'em, and I laid out all the notes I'd made during jury duty. And it was one of those times when a real professional writer knows he's got only one choice: humor. So I stayed up all night writing a lighthearted little satire I called "I, the Juror." Darned if I was going to get left out of Mom and Pop's first issue.

"The funniest thing I've read in I don't know how long," wrote back Mom. "It made me laugh so hard, your father reinjured his knee just running out to the kitchen to see what was the matter."

"Simple, but so well done, it stays funny for me," said the old man, obviously too strong a dad to even mention the pain he must have been in. "I only wish we could count on more like this from you."

"So topical and original, and with so many funny, on-the-inside-looking-out legal observations, that I'm proud to be able to call you my nephew," said Uncle Foster, whom maybe I'd been a little harsh on before.

The next comment in the letter came from Norv, Margie's river-guiding ex-husband, whom I've never even met. He wrote that he and Margie had reconciled, and that he was crashing in my old room at my folks' with her until guiding picked up again and they got remarried. Then he wrote, "But about your piece . . . well, once upon a time, I wrote for an outboard-motor magazine. And as a professional, I couldn't help finding your jury-duty piece thin and shallow. Nothing you'd need an electronic depth-finder to 'get.' (Ha.) Also, the whole business where you jurors are split as to what you want on the pizza never really panned out for me. (Ha ha.) So it gets a great big *no way* from me."

"I can't help agreeing with Norv, I'm afraid," followed up Margie. "It *is* thin—really thin, and a pretty unfunny mess with no hint of control, confidence, or knowledge of the inner workings of our court system. I can hardly believe that this was written by the same brother who taught me how to balance on his bongo board. Sorry. Hey, can you make it to our wedding?"

"Hi. We've never met, but I'm Cart, Norv's best friend" is the way the last comment began. "I'm a river guide working out of the same outfit as Norv, so that's how we met. Right now, though, what with black smoke pouring out from the dump fire upstream, it's been impossible to guide anybody anyplace. So your very generous folks said I could set up shop in their attic for the time being, and use your old rolltop desk to polish up a poem about tricky river currents they want for their first issue. About your jury-duty story, though, I have to agree with Norv and your sister. 'Thin,' they both said? Well, I think they were being kind. Sorry. And sorry, too, from your folks, who've asked me to reject your piece for them. They want you to know that they still like a lot of it anyway, and will always be proud of you, but that they can't publish anything getting this kind of three for–three against vote. But hey—are you coming to Norv and Margie's wedding? Perhaps we'll chew the fat more then."

Now, don't get me wrong. I mean, my mom and dad will always be *my* mom and dad. But I think I've evolved enough emotionally now to start concentrating more on magazines that aren't . . . well, that aren't such little mom-and-pop magazines. Every so often, though, I should probably call home.

The Volunteer Organist

So I'm just leaning back in church Sunday. Blue sunlight is beaming down from the stained-glass window to my side, zeroing in on a barbecue-sauce spill on my gray flannels. It's also warming up my whole right thigh at the expense of the rest of me. But really, I'm pretty comfy, just holding down my pew's red cushioning. Reverend Newitt, who looks so much like one of those "60 Minutes" guys whose name I can never remember, is delivering his sermon. He *sounds* more like some no-nonsense football commentator. And the way he's just accelerated into something like a touchdown run is like my unofficial two-minute warning on his sermon. Honestly, though, I couldn't tell you what Newitt's been preaching about if my ever again eating cold ribs for breakfast depended on it. I'm not snoozing—swear to God—but 90 percent of the old gray matter is just drifting off to

wherever it wants to. I'm way out there someplace, thinking about this old high-school buddy of mine, Cliff. No
reason in particular I'm dwelling on old Cliff, except it
came up recently how he was married with two kids and
was still selling preemergence weed killer.

Long time ago, Cliff brought along a stapled shut
SuperValu grocery bag to the movies and put it up against
my ear. I could hear some walking around in there. Inside,
Cliff tells me when I can't guess, is this little sparrow he
caught. I should have made Cliff free it right away, but
I hesitated, then never said anything, and regretted it later.
I can't recall exactly what the movie was; I know it was
Dracula's Something. What I do remember is this one
scene where a swarm of bats swoops down the chimney to
a big mansion and then they show them dive-bombing
people inside at a big, ritzy party. Right then Cliff opened
his grocery bag. I never thought he'd do it, I guess. And
wouldn't you know, the first thing that bird does is to fly
right for all the light. The poor thing starts flapping against
the movie screen like crazy—like it was trapped in a
screen porch. Well, the folks in the theater went nuts.
Lots of screaming and commotion. Lots of ducking and
lots of women quick covering their hair with both hands
and some men doing it, too.

So I'm sitting next to my wife, Donna, in the middle
of a hundred and some churchgoers, all involved with that
sparrow. Then I become aware that the reverend's voice
has vanished and that the church is quiet. But if Reverend
Newitt has wrapped up his sermon, where the hell, I
wonder, is the almighty blast from the organ that's always
signaled as much?

Snapping back to the here-and-now, I lean over as if

I'm retying my right desert boot when really I'm just making sure that the organ is still there. Well, of course it is; it's still up front, up behind Reverend Newitt's pulpit, where it'll probably be long after every one of us in the congregation has checked out for good. But nobody's sitting under the light at the keyboard, and that's odd. Where's Rose, with the Vince Lombardi build and a wig and the extra-wide red robe, who pumped out the hymn "All Things Bright and Beautiful" before the sermon?

Then Reverend Newitt says, "Rose Kilander, our fine organist, became ill during this morning's service, so we'll have to forgo the singing of the final hymn, 'We Gather Together.' Unless, of course"—and this just has to be an audible—"someone else will volunteer to play for us."

Well, that shoots a little adrenaline through the congregation, spreading some anxious looks over the faces. Who'd ever volunteer to walk up to that mighty Wurlitzer and play the last hymn? Everyone is dying to see.

I don't care if I could've played the organ the day I was born—I *still* wouldn't have volunteered. I couldn't take all the attention—plus, it might have been sacrilegious for someone like me to play. I mean, I'm not a true churchgoer. Far from it. See, my wife, Donna, who hasn't missed a Sunday since I've known her, decided to start dragging me along last year, to "better our relationship," as she put it. And to keep the peace, I didn't fight it. After all, she did come to a slew of demolition derbies this summer without throwing any snit fits. (She kept busy with her nail-lengthening kit at every single one.) So would you believe I've missed only *one* church service in the past few months? (There was an unusual set of circumstances that day: a wild-card berth at stake, an early kickoff, and a brand-new color TV with such a mammoth screen they had to take it apart and bring it into the house in six sections.)

To me, of course, most of church is a lot of mumbo jumbo, no offense. But like I said, I haven't put up any resistance. Because right away I noticed I was getting some excellent thinking done there. And *that* was my single biggest revelation about churchgoing: the big space, the peace and quiet, the choir, that sportscaster's voice, and especially the organ—all of that would lull me into such an incredibly relaxed state that I could drift off like no other time all week.

SO ANYWAY, Reverend Newitt is up there nearly sweating through his black robe, and it's no wonder—he's kind of overcommitted himself to finding a volunteer by this point. "Don't be shy, people," he says, and the place hushes down more than ever. "Isn't there *anyone* here today who'll help us by playing the hymn?" And soon he's staring down the choir, a little desperately, his eyes saying, "*Aren't you folks supposed to be the musical ones?*"

Already trudging down center aisle, though, is an honest-to-goodness bum. He's got on a dark suit, but the thing's creased like an accordion. A sleeve is torn from the elbow down, exposing the sleeve of something like a pajama top. This guy doesn't look Social Security age, but his stringy hair and wild beard are genuine grandpa gray. He carries himself toward the organ with lots of determination, but carefully, too, like his shocks really need replacement. I mean, it's like the guy just came off a bender.

Newitt is plenty weirded out to see this character in his church. He keeps adjusting his round glasses like it's their fault he's seeing what he's seeing. Finally, he hurries out of his pulpit and plants himself directly in front of the organ. And you can't tell right away if he's going to welcome this bum or make some kind of goal-line stand. I'm sure not drifting now; I'm 100 percent present, and as tensed as everybody else.

When the bum reaches Newitt, the reverend forces out a smile, backs off slightly, and motions him to sit down on the organ bench. And when the volunteer hits a couple of warm-up chords, Donna, me, and the rest of the congregation stand and flip through our hymnals to the last hymn.

That turns out to be less important, though, when the bum starts playing a note-perfect seventh-inning stretch. It's funny, and for maybe five seconds, some of us guys in the congregation have to summon up an awful lot of control not to just start stamping instinctively. But then Newitt gets back over, grabs the bum by the arm, and starts pulling him off the bench. It's pretty definitely an unnecessary roughness call. And while part of me sympathizes with the reverend's desire to keep control, the rest of me is thinking about how this guy is harmless and apparently miserable, and if it's going to make him feel even the tiniest bit better to have an audience listen to him noodle around on the organ for a few minutes, it's worth it, it just is. So before any part of me can stop it, I get my hand up to my mouth, megaphone-style, and blurt out, "LET THE MAN PLAY!" Donna squeezes me so hard I think her nails are going to break off in my arm. Reverend Newitt startles, then backs off like a dog caught eating a steak set out to thaw on the counter. And the bum goes right back to working the keys and pedals. And what comes out this time isn't the seventh-inning anymore and it isn't the scheduled hymn, either. It's a very bittersweet melody—stirring, actually, coming as it does from our volunteer—and lots of women in the congregation start sniffling, and, yeah, some men change their positions in the pews and refold their arms a couple of times. You can almost imagine that this guy is playing out his life story for you on the organ, and even though I didn't listen to Reverend Newitt's sermon, no way can it come close to the lesson being put out by this life's example on the bench.

He doesn't play for long. Soon he's walking back up center aisle, head down, with the whole congregation stiller than the casualties I saw once at the Gettysburg Wax Museum. Reverend Newitt stands up in the pulpit and says softly, "Good people, let us pray." And I don't exactly pray then, I don't believe. But I do shut my eyes and let myself go off again.

The Park Avenue Social Review Visits the Drought Dinner in Eagle Grove, Iowa

O N E can never be sure what one will find in roving about Iowa, but if you stumbled into last Saturday's Drought Dinner in Eagle Grove, you were attending the undisputed attention getter of this late, dry season—a time when cornering VIPs of any persuasion is usually something else again.

Spotted in Saturday's super socialite crowd were the likes of Mack Hanson, the electric-pump-repair tycoon; the Olaf Olsens, who have that fantastic Apache fold-down camper with zip-on screen house canopy; unflappable Floyd and Thelma Koolish; Edwin Henkins, who breezed into town fresh from the National Livestock Show in Chicago, where he also picked up a devastatingly simple but elegant work shirt for his sporty wife, Darleen, the noted home-canning wiz; the Elmer Skecktons; and on and on.

The entire affair was held at Gil's, a charmingly primitive yet strikingly romantic steak house near Old Grant Road—still *the* place to be seen and to see in busy Eagle Grove. Poultry farmers especially love Gil's intimate atmosphere—it is an up! And Saturday it managed to attract many from the more refined livestock-breeder set. On tap were Tom Pruder; charming Jack Challio; and, of course, Wally Beezner (it was SRO, but Wally managed to get a table; leave it to Wally!).

Before dinner, guest speaker Lyle Sides, a suave South Dakota beef feeder, talked about the expected feed value of drought-stricken corn silage (with and without ears). While he spoke, Myrtle Lawson—in sporty black denim—slipped in, causing heads to turn. Her husband, Bernie, is Mr. Big in roofing and siding for Boone County.

The dinner that followed was scrumptious: the lovely dishes all keyed to the sophisticated and *all* topped with liberal portions of Gil's famous potato salad. That dynamite deputy Red Winkel (who's still taking bids on the installation of plumbing fixtures in the county jail) was overheard to say that Gil's jumbo fries are among the largest he's ever encountered. That's something, coming from a man who once took first in the tractor pull at the state fair and an hour later outate everyone at the annual Moose Lodge Fish Fry.

Also on hand to enjoy the fine menu were marvelous June Bowden; delightful Charlie and Bev Yankton; Ray Wilcox, the highly acclaimed pest exterminator and bon vivant currently coaching the Goose Lake High Bobcats baseball team; Oscar Depew, a good friend from Skunk River; the dapper conservationalist, Ward Grody—just in from Des Moines, where he was granted additional state funds to determine pheasant population trends in the northern parts of the state as opposed to those in the southern parts; Mel Turmer, with some exciting new plans for an oil-heated chick brooder up his sleeve; and, much to everyone's surprise, Wayne and Esther Rupnow. The Rupnows still reside in that attractive turkey farm on the south side of (new) U.S. 90. Insiders say the Rupnows are still upset over the number of semi drivers using their road to get around the U.S. 90 weigh station. Lay off, boys!

CONSPICUOUSLY absent from the Drought Dinner were the Ralph Zumbachs, currently honeymooning about the Council Bluffs area in their new used 1970 Rollohome mobile trailer (12′ x 30′) with heat. What a wonderful couple they are!

AFTER dinner, the chic-est of those in attendance dashed to the floor to dance and carry on to the superb banjo-and-fiddle stylings of clever Tom and Terri Kanton, the "Bronco Twins." Others (including lovely Mildred Cooper in the unbeatable team of navy blue and white) drifted over to the other end of Gil's for the auctioning off of a ton of high-grade bailing wire—the entire proceeds of which will go to Bob Bilks, who is being hit the hardest by the drought and who also lost his poultry feeder in last month's lively little twister. Of course, Bob was beaming. To him it was a most happy night. And among those adding to his happiness were Chuck Ules of the American Chick Sexing Association and Dody Fisher, the coordinator for the Miss Black Iowa Pageant to be held next month in Fort Dodge.

NO SOONER was the auction over than the sky began to rumble, the lights at Gil's flickered, and the rains came. Which only proved, once again, that a large dinner dance with the right mix can be the surest remedy for a lingering drought. We loved it!

Something the Matter with Dad

J U S T before I left home to start college, I did something pretty dumb to the ring I got for being one of last swim season's high-school state champions. I stormed into the family room, this was Labor Day evening, and dropped it—my 400-meter-backstroke ring—through the little metal doors in the bottom of the fireplace. It wasn't the most adult thing to do. I mean, if I'd taken out my frustration some other way, maybe by swimming White Bear Lake across and back in the dark, I'd be using the ring now to talk to more girls in the dorm. But at the time, I didn't care *what* happened to it: I was all upset still from what had happened earlier that Labor Day, when I'd washed Dad's car—or *thought* I'd washed it.

I started out on that Monday holiday eating raisin toast and just staring out the kitchen window toward the driveway; that's when I got the bright idea about washing

Dad's Futura. See, I hoped that my cleaning it would lure Dad outdoors for a change, and that that might, somehow, inspire him to drive me up to college the next morning—even though his temperamental behavior this summer made all that a real long shot. My high-school swimming coach, Coach Kern, had offered to take me and all my stuff up in his minivan. But it was really important to me, for a lot of reasons, to have Dad drive me.

Dad used to keep his car looking brand new. Soon as he got home from his weekly tour of our tri-state area (his territory for selling lead-lined X-ray aprons to dentists), he'd go right to work on all the grime and bug juice. But ever since his and Mom's big blowout on the Fourth of July—it ended with Mom moving into the house across the street and Dad staying home on an extended breather from lead-apron sales—his Futura had just been collecting dust in the driveway. So, anyway, on Labor Day morning, before I ten-speeded over to White Bear Lake for my last lifeguarding shift of the summer, I scrubbed Dad's car real hard. Once I had it back to showroom-white, I pulled my swim goggles down around my neck (they kept soap out of my eyes) and went inside to rouse Dad.

Well, the TV was on in the den, as usual. And I found Dad in there, of course, lying in his recliner in just his pajama bottoms. He had Triscuits smeared with mint jelly laid out on a tray on his stomach (when Mom left, so did normal meals), and he was watching another one of his Mitchum movies. Two whole bookshelves of the den were *just* Robert Mitchum movies. (According to Mom, everyone used to tell Dad that he looked like

Robert Mitchum, which he does, in the old photo albums.) In the western Dad was watching, Mitchum had on his usual one-tough-hombre expression. He was lifting his heavy eyelids and saying to another cowboy, "Try it and I'll whack you between the horns." I cut in and asked Dad to step outside for a second. He didn't respond. "It's about your car," I said. Finally, in a you'll-be-sorry tone, I said, "It's never looked better." Dad paused his movie with the remote then, and led the way out to the driveway. I hoped Mom was using her binoculars from the house across the street: the more often she spied Dad outside and acting close to normal (she'd said to me over the phone), the better the chances were she'd move back home. This time, though, I did try to screen her from seeing Dad in partial jammies.

After a thorough inspection of his Futura, Dad sighed and said, "Doesn't look like those goggles do your eyes any favors." He started pointing out all these places I'd missed —like the antenna, the little depressions beneath all the door handles, the windshield-wiper arms, the enclosed part of the "6" on the rear license plate, and the inside of the gas-tank door, of all the stupid places. And that's when my 400-meter-backstroke ring came up: "This scratch on the hood," Dad said, running his finger along something resembling a hair, "that's definitely something new." Then, nodding toward my ring, he said, "Do me a big favor next time, fella, and remove your jewelry *first*."

SOMETHING was noticeably out of whack with Dad in May. For one thing, see, he always used to insist on mowing the lawn himself. He called it his "thinking time," and he'd be out there twice every week, mowing and thinking. So I knew something weird was up right after I graduated, when Dad cut the grass two days in a row—then not for ten days—then two days in a row—then not for three weeks. But Mom said it was nothing. She told me that Dad, in fact, had recently gotten some very *good* news: his lead-apron firm had picked a young assistant to help Dad on his tri-state swings this fall. Okay, but then how come, in addition to Dad's erratic mowing, his driving started to become so temperamental? He became obsessed with passing other cars, especially the sporty models. His Futura could really move, it was true, but that didn't make it any more relaxing to be his passenger. Also, Dad started surging ahead if a car made a move to pass him. During a lift he gave me to White Bear Lake beach, he punched it up to ninety-five to keep a Porsche behind us. I said, "You're asking for an expensive ticket." He shot me a Robert Mitchum–like "What's it to you?" look and laughed me off, boasting that the lead-apron samples piled in his trunk would "outfox any lawman's radar gun." Mom had no more reaction to Dad's driving than she'd had to Dad's mowing. But she did start finding rides home from her evening yoga classes, instead of calling and having Dad pick her up. When I pressed her about that change, she finally admitted that Dad's fuse *had* shortened, but said I shouldn't worry, insisting it was simply a "temporary re-action to the strong aerosol adhesive" he'd used to replace some tiles in the bathroom shower. Supposedly, he hadn't read the part about adequate ventilation until afterwards. But if whatever was the matter with Dad was so temporary, then how come Dad *still* seemed agitated in July, and started the big Fourth of July scene with Mom, which led to her moving across the street?

B A C K on the Fourth, at White Bear Lake, Dad and Mom and I were waiting for the fireworks to start, sitting quietly on a raggedy old electric blanket. We had all kinds of time till the display, too, because Dad had driven over so fast. While Mom and I were gradually untensing, a lanky guy with a blond, braided ponytail showed up and knelt on our blanket in front of Mom. (I scooted back until I was stuck sitting on the blanket's plug.) The guy's braid hung forward, down to the gold cord around the waist of his jeans, and he had several gold hoops through one ear. He put his hands on Mom's shoulders, gently pulled her forward, and kissed her on the forehead. Mom was blushing when she introduced him to me and Dad. This was the "Kress" we'd heard so much about at home, Mom's yoga instructor from her adult-ed classes. He had amazing green eyes—Mom hadn't been kidding us about that part. He seemed like a nice enough guy, and shook my hand with both of his. He checked out my gold-plated 400-meter-backstroke ring; he said he'd heard all about my swimming from Mom. When he asked about my plans, I told him about my athletic scholarship to college. Then he wanted to know if I'd ever tried meditating before swim meets—"You know," he said, "to focus your mind." Soon, he was giving me the business card of his friend who teaches meditation here, just off campus. Well, it turned out to be a pretty long huddle that Mom and I had gotten into with Kress; he had one of those soothing voices you were content to just keep listening to. He was praising Mom and her progress in yoga when the first burst from the night's display lit up his face red. Before he took off, Kress kissed Mom on her hand. And if it seemed a little too affectionate to me, I could only wonder how it looked to Dad.

As far as the fireworks show went—well, right away I missed the enormous exploding chrysanthemums that they'd shot off the previous summer. This year's display had too many little twinkling doodads, and some duds, too. One skyrocket trailing red sputtered halfway up, then surged downward and spiraled into the lake. Dad—and this was really sarcastic—yelled, "Wow!" Nobody around us laughed. And soon, when one lonesome aerial shell only puffed into something like a weak little dandelion, Dad went, "*Oooooooh!*"—really exaggerating it. I glanced over to see if Mom was as embarrassed as I was; she didn't look any too happy.

It was an awfully quiet ride home until Dad gunned the Futura past a truck on a bridge. Then Mom started waving a ten-dollar bill in the air. "Dairy Queen—on me!" she announced, trying to change the mood. Dad really stomped on it past the Dairy Queen, though: he didn't seem to want the young smoochers in the convertible behind us to pass him by. And that did it for Mom. She started scolding Dad for what a childish thing that was, but Dad came right back with no, childish was what it was when there's someone her age taking yoga. Dad said that for her to pay for yoga lessons from "Master Ponytail" was the same as throwing money away. "It's like this," he said, snatching the ten out of Mom's hand and letting it fly out his window. Well, afraid of what might happen next, I flopped down across the backseat, closed my eyes tight, and tried meditating myself right out of the car. But soon

I heard Dad getting back into it with Mom, in low, harsh whispers: something about Mom and a guy slow-dancing at a wedding. Dad claimed it went on for a full twelve-and-a-half minutes. So what? Mom said—it was her second cousin. The whole thing got me feeling so unhappy, I just punched my leg as hard as I could, and it hurt.

When I finally got home and shut the door to my room—well, there was something seriously the matter with me then, because even though there wasn't any big swim meet the next day, I went into the bathroom and shaved my head anyway. It wasn't the most mature thing to do. But I couldn't have cared less at the time.

A F T E R the dramatics on the Fourth, Mom didn't waste any time arranging to rent the bungalow across the street. It had sat empty for two years, never attracting any buyers because of what was supposed to be a permanent pet odor, starting in the kitchen. And after Mom moved over, Dad quit driving altogether. He mostly kept to the house, sleeping a lot, watching and rewatching his Robert Mitchum movies, and eating miscellaneous food combinations out of the fridge—usually involving junk from the door. He completely quit mowing the lawn after Mom left, too—I guess eating herring tidbits while watching Mitchum carouse around Hong Kong with a bar girl was like Dad's *new* thinking time. So I decided to take over the mowing. I did more worrying than thinking while I mowed. I worried about Dad, of course; I worried that Dad's behavior was going to keep Mom, who I also worried about, living out at binocular range; and I even worried about stuff like the vibrations coming off our trembly old mower:

as soon as I took over the mowing, the thing started this wild routine of sputtering, then recovering, then sputtering some more, then surging, over and over. Eventually it would settle into a very rough *putt-putt,* and that always left my hands feeling Novocained for a full half-hour after finishing the lawn, even though I wore wet-suit mitts lent to me by Coach Kern *over* Dad's three-ply cowhide yard gloves. My real worry was that all that constant shaking traveling up my arm would throw an elbow out of whack, and keep me off the college swim team—maybe even end with them tearing up my scholarship. I tried tinkering with the mower, but if anything I made it worse. Still, I kept the yard neat, in spite of fizzy hands—for Mom. Until I finally had to leave for college in September, I was determined to keep it looking halfway decent.

I MISSED Mom, and told her so over the phone in July and August, but I never went across to visit. I just didn't want to see her till she was back home. Deep down I was mad at her for leaving me stuck with Dad midway through the summer, and also, I suppose, for feeding me that dumb toxic-tile-stickum explanation for what had to be some kind of age crisis Dad was going through. During one phone talk I had with Mom in August, she said she'd be a lot closer to moving home when Dad came out from being holed up indoors and started acting more like the regular, mostly even-tempered guy we used to know. And I was beginning to think that getting Dad out might also improve my chances for a ride to school in September.

So on one of the first of the cool summer nights I tried tempting Dad into an outside excursion by casually mentioning a new rib joint that had opened nearby. I tried not to oversell the place; I knew I didn't have to, since ribs were Dad's number one food anyway. And sure enough, he pulled on some jeans I'd never seen before—they had lots of fancy stitching on the pockets—and we left the house together for dinner. On the way to eat, I pointed out to Dad how all the fireflies' lights had dimmed considerably, meaning, I said, that fall was almost here. He still didn't suddenly offer to drive me up to school, though. In fact, he seemed almost jealous, and I wondered if it had something to do with him having such a good time as a Delta-something-something when he was my age.

The waitress who brought us menus was Patti Winther, one of the real knockouts from high school. Most of the swim team had had a crush on her, partly because she wasn't too stuck-up. The first thing she did after coming over to our booth was to skim the top of my head with her hand. It made me blush. I was still recuperating from my July scalping; my hair was boot-camp length. Patti asked me how my summer was going. "Okay," I lied. I caught her looking at my state champion backstroke ring. Then, before I could finish a quick Patti-Dad, Dad-Patti intro, Dad cut in and said, "Jesus Christ, you know every great-looking babe!" He gave Patti the wink then, like some guy who had pretty much seen it all. I tried to distract Patti from his man-of-the-world act by asking about her fall plans. Not only was she going up to college—turns out she was staying at Aberdeen Hall, too.

"We're in the same dorm, then," I said to Patti.

"The same dorm!" Dad cut in, shaking his gray head like he'd heard me wrong. I had to tell him that yes, Aberdeen Hall was going coed this year. His eyelids immediately drooped down, one-tough-hombre style. "Boy, there's something *we* never had," he said, kind of crossly. "Of course, I wouldn't have got much studying done," he right away bragged, while attempting to nudge Patti in the side but actually elbowing her squarely on the breast. It had to have smarted, but she pretended that it hadn't even happened. I went kind of numb then, and spent the rest of dinner staring out at the squirrels getting ready for fall.

The next morning, I picked up the phone to call Patti. I wanted to apologize, and, depending on how that went, I was planning on asking her to stop by White Bear Lake and sit up in the lifeguard stand with me. While I was dialing, though, I realized I didn't know how I'd explain Dad's rib-restaurant behavior. For a moment I even thought about blaming that heady tile glue. Then I convinced myself that Patti was going to say no thanks to the whole White Bear Lake part, and that someone as cute as she was wouldn't want to hang out with someone like me anyway. So why bother complicating things? I told myself, and hung up right after Patti answered.

COACH Kern called at the end of August. Someone had told him about my off-season skinhead, and he sounded concerned and a lot less coachlike than usual. When he asked if I needed anything, I came right out and asked him if he'd mind driving me up to college. It was reassuring to know I'd have a ride no matter what, but I *still* kept thinking about having Dad take me up. Which explains my desperation shot, the failed car-wash attempt, last week.

The morning after Labor Day, I slipped into the den, where Dad was lying around in cutoffs. He was eating breakfast and watching Robert Mitchum keep going back for more in a saloon brawl. I didn't have anything to lose at that point. "Coach Kern is coming over for me soon," I said. "To take me up." Dad didn't say anything, just kept his eyes on the TV while he finished what smelled like a horseradish sandwich. "He's got one of those sporty new minivans," I said. "It's so roomy—I bet it'll hold all my school stuff." Still nothing from Dad. Then, finally, it just came out. "Listen, Dad," I said. "If you could be the one to drive me to school today, instead of . . . well, it'd really mean a lot to me, you know." And all I can figure is that my straight-shooting, no-nonsense approach must have caught Dad with his guard down, because pretty soon he stopped his movie and led the way out to the driveway to his mostly clean Futura.

"Okay, chum," Dad said to me, "okay." He sprung open the trunk with his key. He still seemed pretty distracted, but at least he was there for me. After Dad and I had removed all his lead-lined-apron samples, Dad bragged he had enough trunk space to "run guns to the rebels," and I wondered which Mitchum movie *that* was from. Later, while Dad and I were loading in cartons of my school stuff, I saw some movement in the draperies across the street: Mom, probably taking everything in through her binoculars.

SURE, I wish everything at home had been settled before I left. I don't like worrying about Dad now while I'm trying to swim my fastest-ever heats. And I hate suddenly wondering how things are between Dad and Mom while I'm trying to answer an essay question on a psych quiz. But there still isn't much I can do about it. There *is* something I can do for myself, though: something that hit me plain as day this afternoon, while working out in the big college pool. I kept getting this odd sensation: it felt like I had my 400-meter-backstroke ring on again. I even slowed down and put my hand up to my goggles to check. All I was feeling, of course, was the cold water on my finger's newly exposed band of skin. And this ring feeling in the pool today reminded me how I never actually destroyed my ring. So, when I eventually do visit home again, like at Thanksgiving, there's nothing to stop me from going behind the furnace in the basement with a flashlight, opening the metal door to the ash pit, sifting through the ashes, and—I hope—coming out of the basement wearing my state champ ring again.

What the Twister Did

THIS morning while Daryl Eckner was equalizing my sideburns with his electric clippers, I thought I saw the ring pull from a window shade hanging down from his glasses. At first, it was just dangling down in front of his face, but it started dancing around when Daryl said to me, about the big tornado that hit us a while back, "It could have been worse." Then, just like all the other weird things I'd seen since that tornado, the ring pull was gone.

Daryl was right: it could have been a whole lot worse. Because what the big Palm Sunday twister *didn't* do, fortunately, was harm any man, woman, or child here. But that was probably only because our heroic ham-radio operators got such speedy advance warnings out around town. And the fact that we all have good, strong storm cellars didn't hurt, either. After that, we were just plain lucky, I guess, because when the big twister lifted (Dad always used to say they can take off as quickly as they land), and people came out of hiding and started looking over the damage to their homes, property, and livestock, the old-timers in town agreed that the twister had been pretty nasty.

It seemed nasty to me, too, even though it was my first experience with one. But there was something else about it. I mean, I didn't have to survey what was left of Mom's and my home and belongings or of my bicycle-repair shop in the barn for very long to understand why people always call tornadoes mischievous. Because you know what the big twister did? It yanked the little man off the top of my horseshoes trophy (seven years ago, in high school, I pitched a pretty accurate shoe) and blew him right into a small 7-Up bottle. Didn't even disturb the right arm he's got cocked back. And you know where we finally found the bottle? Inside one of Mom's empty hatboxes. (Ever since Dad passed on, it seems Mom can't collect enough empty cardboard boxes.) And that turned up in the front seat of my Jeep, which was discovered about two-thirds of a mile down the road from our place, sitting on top of the Metcalfs' silo, where the dome had been.

Now, if that had been the tornado's only weird trick on us, it wouldn't have seemed so remarkable. But there was a lot more. Take the big Swiss army knife I kept in my top bureau drawer. I found it inside the grass-seed spreader, which had its T-shaped handle stuck through one of the holes of the big birdhouse, which was still sitting undisturbed on its pole in our front yard. And all the blades and tools on the knife were flipped out—same as in the poster they used to have taped up in the window at the hardware store—minus the fish scaler/hook disgorger, which was gone completely. The next week, when the insurance agent was going around the place with me, *that* showed up, with the starter rope from the lawn mower wrapped around it, inside the banjo Dad made for me, from a locally grown gourd, when I was born.

The twister didn't pick on just me and Mom, though. It was to blame for similar "jokes" all over town. Frank Nisswa, the half-Sioux whose farm is on the opposite side of town from us, said the tornado sucked all the water out of his well and carried his china cabinet eight hundred yards before setting it down again in his cornfield, without breaking a single cup or dish. And Frank told me that inside, sitting on top of a stack of dinner plates, he found the vise that had been clamped to his workbench. Yvette Kenner, one of those courageous ham-radio operators I mentioned before, said that she and her boyfriend and her twins came out of their storm cellar expecting the very worst, but all they found was their electronic fun organ's bossa-nova beat playing and their parakeet plucked clean of feathers but otherwise okay. And Daryl Eckner himself, barber and captain of They Might Be Gods, our State Champion tug-of-war team, has told everyone over and over how he climbed out of his cellar to find that the traveling van, with the team's name painted in fancy circus lettering on both sides, which was normally parked in his backyard, had vanished. It hasn't shown up yet. According to Daryl, a spiderweb between the legs of his barbecue— only twenty feet from where the van had been sitting— hadn't been touched. All there was, he said, was the purple foil wrapping from an Easter candy stuck in the middle.

Word of what the big twister did must have gotten out fast, because a man in a red beret—some sort of carnival big shot—showed up during our cleanup. In no time, with the help of our eager ham-radio operators, he had the news out that he'd be setting up a tent where the self-service car wash used to be, and was ready to pay cash for our "tornado curiosities." Even before he got all the tent stakes in the ground he bought Chet Rittie's shotgun-with-seven-blades-of-straw-and-a-mascara-applicator-driven-into-the-stock, and Herman Joplin's phone-receiver-embedded-in-the-leaf-from-a-dinner-table, and Gladys Wells's sneaker-lodged-inside-a-twenty-foot-length-of-hose.

I wonder if it was really that great an idea to be pitching easy money around a town in such disrepair, where everyone's state aid and insurance money was still two weeks away. It was tempting to me, I know, since it came right when I needed cash to get the crane to come in and take my Jeep down off the Metcalfs' silo. I didn't want to sell my horseshoe-pitcher-in-the-7-Up-bottle, though. How many times is a guy—even a guy living in twister country—going to get ahold of a keepsake like that? So, several nights running, once Mom was asleep (it seems she can't sleep enough since Dad passed on), I did something I'm not proud of: I fashioned my *own* twister jokes. I figured the carnival guy wouldn't know the difference, and maybe I'd get my Jeep down.

It wasn't easy, what with half my bicycle-repair tools scattered who knows where, but after a few sleepless nights in the barn I'd assembled quite a group of "authentic" twister curiosities. There was the half-a-bowling-ball-with-the-bicycle-tire-pump-lodged-in-the-thumbhole. And the tricky ball-of-piano-wire-and-salad-forks-and-umbrella-skeleton-and-bicycle-spokes-jammed-inside-a-big-goldfish-bowl. And my favorite, which I really wished I could keep—the ice-cream-scoop-coming-out-of-bongos-with-gardening-shears-going-in. Well, the carnival man really went for them—he even whistled when he first picked up the bowling-ball thing. And so I hired the crane for a hundred and seventy-five dollars *and* kept my man-in-the-bottle.

But about two months after the big twister, I put him in one of Mom's empty shoe boxes that still had the white tissue in it and buried it. I didn't need it anymore to know how weird things could be after a tornado, because even though our town was pretty much back together, I couldn't walk down Center Street without, for a moment, seeing some kind of twister curiosity mirage, like a lampshade on a fire hydrant, or the float ball from a toilet tank drifting across a big puddle. And once I even thought I saw Mom's rocker, which we never did find, hooked upside down on the town-hall clock. I even planned how I would wait for the hand to lower to twenty after the hour and catch the thing when it slid off. But it disappeared at ten past. The worst time had to be when I was driving home in my res-cued Jeep, with the annoying new whine it makes over thirty, to share some homemade soup with Mom and finish replacing the shingles. I glanced up at the top of the Metcalfs' silo, where the new dome was under way, and for just a moment I saw myself up there in my Jeep on twister-lookout, with a portable ham radio on my knees and my half-a-pair-of-binoculars around my neck.

This condition let up all last week, but this morning, in the barber chair, there was that damn ring pull swing-ing from Daryl Eckner's glasses. It didn't last long, though, and next thing I knew Daryl was going on and on about the upcoming dance that's supposed to raise money for our tug-of-war team's new van. "We're all bouncing back now, huh?" Daryl said, spinning me around to look at myself in the mirror. And I saw a largemouth bass on my head—until Daryl spun me back a hundred and eighty degrees from the mirror, and I realized it was just the old prizewinner that had always been mounted on Daryl's wall. And tonight, while reorganizing the hall closet, I came across the fancy Sunday bonnet Mom used to wear to church before she started sleeping through the bells. I almost yanked the long peacock feather from under the hatband, but then I realized that that was exactly where it belonged. So while I'm hoping that the ring pull was the last of my mirages, I'm beginning to wonder now if I'll ever again see anything the way I used to.

The Long Donut Hole

A SHINY red compact with the dealer's sticker in the left rear window pulled up to the Long Donut Hole this morning. It was a Dodge Colt, one of those little sporty-but-practical numbers they show swerving around traffic cones in the classier car magazines. We've never had one here before. I got off my stool and walked over, assuming it was just another out-of-towner who'd ask me for a half-dozen, say, cinnamon donuts. See, it looks like we still sell donuts at the Long Donut Hole, and every day I have to give a few passers-through-town the bad news. Today, though, when this Colt's window hummed down, there was old Claude Geterson. I couldn't believe it. I said, "Claude!" But then I wasn't sure what to say. It was real awkward: Claude and I had already exchanged lengthy good-byes at his little retirement bash only two weeks before. (In fact, we're still working on a

leftover case of beer.) So I was just staring at Claude,
wondering what on earth had brought him back so soon. I
mean, I hadn't seen any favorite jacket of his lying around
or anything. But before I get any further into this morning's visit from Claude, I should explain about the Long
Donut Hole and the job I have here now. (It beats working the graveyard shift at an upstate windshield-wiper
factory—the first job I had after dropping out of junior
college.)

YOU'D have to be driving through this town blindfolded
to miss the Long Donut Hole. How else are you not going
to notice two huge brown donut halves set into the ground,

a half a block apart, with a long, low brick building connecting them at the holes? (The driveway running through the length of the building is what makes it the Long Donut Hole.) Of course, these donut-hungry out-of-town types who spot us and drive up expecting to order a dozen, say, powdered sugar, always leave disappointed. Occasionally, though, one of these disappointeds will lean way out his window, check to see how dirty his car is, then maybe decide to travel through the Long Donut Hole anyway. (It's up to them—I don't have to pressure anyone, like I did selling skate guards door-to-door.) Anyway, since Claude retired, it's been my job to get all the cars aligned with the donut-hole entrance. Then, once I've stuffed the folks' three bucks into my change apron, I remind them to put themselves in neutral, turn off their engine, and roll up the windows. Then I hit a button, and they get caught underneath by a big chain and towed the length of the hole for a wash-rinse-blow-dry that has them out the exit donut in sixty seconds, maybe seventy, if they have an outside radio antenna or if Robin, our blow-dry gal, has had her flask of peach brandy working that day—two minutes, call it, for antenna *and* flask.

Claude Geterson spent his last week at the Long Donut Hole grooming me to be his replacement. He also did a lot of reminiscing then about what he called his "donut days." He said that ten years ago, before the place got converted to a car wash, you could drive into the donut hole, purchase a sack of donuts from a uniformed gal behind a window in the middle of the hole, then take off via the exit donut. Claude had spent years and years making all the donuts in a window next to the cashier's. The odd flavor combos he concocted must have been really tasty, because several times during my training week, car-wash customers tapped their horns when they saw Claude and yelled out some of his old combos: "Almond-apple!" they'd shout, or "Strawberry-fudge!" Claude would salute back. I saw one older man roll down his window and yell, "Glazed coconut!" But the guy's timing was so lousy, he got a mouthful of soapy water from one of the automatic sprayers for his trouble.

There just wasn't the opportunity to create anything as memorable as the glazed-coconut donut after the place's transformation to car wash, but Claude did add a few little touches. Take the big, dangling rack of cloth strips that we operate back and forth over hoods, roofs, and trunks, for example. Claude's the one who dyed it crimson and started everyone here calling it Satan's Mop. And the bristly rollers that spin in and scrub the sides of the cars—well, guess who painted them pink and started us referring to them as Your Mother's Curlers? And the big sign at the exit donut that reads IF YOU GET OUT AND LOOK AT YOUR REFLECTION IN YOUR WINDSHIELD AND YOU DON'T LOOK TEN YEARS YOUNGER, CIRCLE AROUND AND GO THROUGH AGAIN—ON US, well, that was one of Claude's little ideas, too, although Stu, our rinse man, who's always in combat fatigues and who's down the hole just before Robin, claims *he* had the idea first.

So, occasionally, I had been imagining how proud Claude would be if he could see me now. For one thing, I'm still here after two weeks, aren't I? (I lasted two *days* running a machine that bent pieces of wire into croquet hoops.) But what I always imagined would make Claude the proudest is how I've become the "new" Claude. Not that I could ever replace Claude himself. But in my first couple of weeks at the Long Donut Hole, I've added some pretty Claude-like touches.

For instance, currently, and at no extra charge, folks going through the wash are welcome to take along our battery-operated cassette player *plus* their choice from a few one-minute self-improvement tapes we have available. That minute they spend sealed up in their cars needn't go to waste any longer. Not when they can be listening to something like "Stop Getting So Angry" or "Overcoming Your Fear of Death" or "I Love My Female Body." And I've also come up with a great public-relations stunt, something I'm surprised Claude never hit on: encouraging wedding parties and funeral processions to drive through the Long Donut Hole anytime, free of charge.

SO ANYWAY, here was old Claude Geterson in the flesh this morning, back only two weeks after his big send-off party and unable to twist himself out of his new plaything's bucket seat without a hand. "It's going okay, Chief," he said to me before I could ask him how it was going. I thought about offering him a cold beer, but didn't: maybe it's bad luck to drink something left over from your own retirement party.

"That's great, Claude," I said, shaking his hand with both of mine. "But what about Atlantic City?" During his final week at the Long Donut Hole, Claude told everyone he was going to move out there and start sitting ringside for the likes of Frank and Cher and some Amazing Kanaldi guy.

"Any day now," Claude said, stuffing his hands deep into the pockets of his overalls. "I'm getting used to having every day off right here, first," he said. "It's always an adjustment, you see, Chief, having every day off. It's great, though . . . having every day off."

"So how you keeping busy?" I asked.

"Oh, there's always a lot of little stuff to take care of," he said, now digging in the front of his mouth with a fancy club-sandwich-type toothpick. "I happen to be extremely busy right now. And it looks like I'll be putting in a few weeks at the Dairy Queen, come December."

"December?" I said.

"Yeah, I'll be selling Christmas trees outta there. Why not?" He shrugged, and the fancy toothpick moved to the other corner of his mouth.

Then a familiar station wagon rolled up: a new regular of ours. "Allow me," Claude said, and he broke into a little trot to get to it. "You take a break," he yelled back over his shoulder. Soon Claude had directed the driver of the wagon up to the donut hole and had collected her money. Then there was trouble. "She won't roll up her window," Claude yelled to me. "Says she wants her tape." So I ran over and gave this gal the cassette player and the "I Want to Remember My Past Lives" tape, the one she always takes. Then I gave Claude the all-clear, and he hit the button, sending her forward into the Long Donut Hole and, I guess, backward into her past life.

"That doesn't seem like such a hot idea," Claude said then. "How do you get the gear back?"

"Robin," I told him. "She'll bring everything back once she's blow-dried the car." Claude didn't say anything. He launched the toothpick sky-high and headed into the donut hole, taking in deep breaths, the soap-and-hot-water mist apparently agreeing with him. I trailed Claude, wondering what he'd say if a funeral procession were to pull in just then.

"Still using Satan's Mop, I see," Claude said proudly, as if a whole two years had gone by instead of two weeks. "You know, I meant to give it another treatment with the red dye before I left—so it'd really come out at you, *whammo!* But . . . hey, who's the new kid?" he suddenly asked, nodding ahead to the teenager I recently put in charge of operating Satan's Mop; see, during Claude's reign, Stu, our rinse man, used to swab cars with the Mop and then he had to run down and operate the rinse, too. But last week I hired my old friend Pete to be in charge of Satan's Mop.

"That's Pete," I yelled over all the racket. "We met up at the windshield-wiper factory." Pete comes to work every day on a skateboard. As he finished mopping the station wagon, Claude headed over to him.

"Pete?" Claude said, offering his hand. "Claude Geterson." Pete pushed his goggles up onto his forehead, smiled, and shook Claude's hand in the arm-wrestling position.

"Heard a lot about you, Mr. Geterson. Heard about your—what was it?—cocoa-ized donut."

"Glazed coconut," Claude said a little sharply. Then, smiling, he said, "Pete, why don't you let me take over here for a second. This station wagon's so filthy you'd better go and hit the flipper switch so's we can get the bottom, too." Claude was obviously dying to get back behind the controls. Pete just laughed, though, and stayed put. We had already pulled our Greenhorn Trick on him.

"I'm not falling for that again, Mr. Geterson," Pete said. "Stu had me looking everyplace for it on my first day." He pulled his goggles back down. Claude half-heartedly patted Pete on the shoulder, then continued through the Long Donut Hole, past Your Mother's Curlers and on down the line toward Stu, on rinse, and Robin, on blow-dry and maybe peach brandy. I didn't go with him. I went back to my stool out front, but had a hard time concentrating on my newspaper.

Some minutes later, Claude emerged from the Long Donut Hole and into daylight. He said to me, "Well, Chief, I don't want to be any more of a bother. You just miss the guys, you know. You miss the craziness."

Claude made me promise then that I'd come by the Dairy Queen in December and got all excited telling me how he was going to treat some of the Christmas trees with tropical-fruit scents. He said he'd have one of these specially "odorized" spruces all ready for me when I showed up. In fact, mine, he told me, would also be pretrimmed with Day-Glo pinecones. So I told him that he shouldn't ever wait for his new Colt to get dirty to show his face. "You come back anytime," I said—it just popped out. But you know, I kind of doubt Claude will be back right away. I think he really needed to hear it, though, regardless.

The Ways We Surfed

CRAWLING up the middle of all four boards in Floyd Miller's surfboard arsenal was a cobra, airbrushed in totally realistic colors by my surfing buddy Doug Kamokuu, originally from Honolulu. Cobras with their hoods flared open had always scared the heck out of Floyd. But all he'd said last May when he'd dropped off his milk-white boards for Doug to airbrush was "They'll get me going this summer." The day after, in the airbrushing room of the surfboard shop Doug and I worked at part-time, Doug, in mid-cobra, confided to me through his old fencing mask that he thought the cobras were a pretty weird way for Floyd to psych himself up; surfers usually wanted their boards to give off *good* vibes. Doug's boards, for instance, had been carefully airbrushed THE WHO or SANTANA or THE HONOLUMONICS. I told Doug I thought there was another reason it was strange: The miraculously consistent six-to-eight-foot swells that made Sherwood Beach one of the most serious surfing experiences on the California coast had always been enough to get Floyd going before.

With the summer weather, then, came what we now call Big Mother's Day, and Floyd, on one of his newly emblazoned boards, was the only surfer foolish enough to paddle out into the twelve-foot mountains of water rolling into Sherwood, courtesy of tropical storm Dwayne. What Doug and I witnessed from the safety of our beach chairs that afternoon was the debut of a new Floyd—not the devoted soul surfer who'd surfed strictly for his own enjoyment of sun, sand, and the fleeting exhilaration of nature's free ride, but a regular kamikaze, carving phenomenal lines into those dangerous walls of water and, in the process, attracting every telephoto lens on the beach. Doug and I finally sulked away from the whole circus. It was hard to deal with all the sudden new attention Floyd was receiving for risking his skeletal structure. And, frankly, as a couple of bona fide soul surfers, we felt a little betrayed.

The next morning, in the sanding room of the surfboard shop, I told Doug through my surgical mask that I had to talk to Floyd right away. The cobras were awesome, I assured Doug, but it wasn't as if they were solely responsible for the suicidal Floyd we'd just witnessed on Big Mother's Day. So that very evening we got Floyd to meet us at our local bar, Ocean Motion, home of the tailless monkeys. Finally, after two frozen Coast Pounders, Floyd *really* started talking. He apologized to me and Doug for what he called his "grandstanding," but said that day after day of surfing just for the "temporary fun" of each wave had started feeling pretty meaningless to him. So, he said, now that he was facing his thirtieth birthday, he'd decided to put himself on the line for something more lasting. He was determined to make it onto the cover of one of the major surfing magazines. And, shortly after that maybe, into a low-budget surfumentary.

Following another round of frozen Coast Pounders, Floyd told us about the recurring dream that he'd been hounded by all last spring. In it, he said, he'd be completely alone in the ocean and "what felt like the whole planet" when the juiciest, bluest, most perfectly shaped wave imaginable would roll in. He'd paddle into position to take off on it; then he'd just let it go by. What was the point of surfing it, he'd feel in the dream, if there wasn't anybody present to document it? Well, Floyd took off for his night job then, leaving Doug and me—twenty-seven and twenty-eight years old, respectively—sitting under the cages full of tailless monkeys, wondering about the way *we* surfed.

AS SUMMER continued, so did Floyd's quest for surf-coverdom, and he got even more radical. In July, on Biggest Monday, the day Sherwood was receiving the industrial-strength aftereffects of a Japanese earthquake, Floyd climaxed his simply berserko afternoon surf session by slaloming in through the dark pilings of the Sherwood Beach pier on a fifteen-foot monster, his left wrist in a cast from the day before, and up to the people oohing and aahing onshore. Max Wong, *Shred* magazine's star photographer, was in that throng, shooting what he thought were yards and yards of Kodachrome. Yards and yards of air were what they turned out to be: Evidently, in his excitement, Max had forgotten to load up. Doug and I, downing nachos and Hawaiian Punch back at the taco stand at the time, had to run down and restrain Floyd.

Like it or not, Floyd's he-man wave riding that summer did nudge Doug and me into some pretty outrageous surfing of our own. For instance, that Tuesday after Biggest Monday, when the waves were down to a saner height, I pulled off my snappiest bottom turns ever atop my PRAY FOR SURF airbrushed twin-fin. And Doug, his wet Hawaiian skin glistening like a coffee bean, steered his THE KINKS needle-nose into a sensationally curling wave that completely enclosed him as it broke, resulting in a lengthy stand-up tube ride that didn't end till he was way north, on the nude beach. Basically, of course, we were still just surfing for the momentary rush we got from our union with each new wave—*not* to make it onto the cover of some surf magazine. And at least we had sensible limits when it came to wave heights. Floyd had none. His scary, big-wave wipeouts frequently got him so cut up by rocks or his own board that the Pipeline column in a new issue of *Surfer* even referred to him as "Floyd 'B-Positive' Miller." That pleased Floyd, though he was quick to point out that the mention was *not* the same thing as a cover.

In August, on the same day Floyd took a spill that required seven stitches in his neck, a new issue of *Wave Rider* appeared on the stands, with Floyd on the pull-out centerfold poster. True, there were three other surfers featured as well (at the top it said "Surfing California"), and it wasn't the most exciting shot of Floyd, but the caption read: "Floyd 'Cobra' Miller—Wave Killer." Still, in Floyd's book it was no substitute for a cover.

Soon after the centerfold had hit the stands, though, Floyd dragged Doug and me to Ocean Motion to give us "really hot news."

"I'm a little nervous," Floyd actually confessed, "but now that it's all set up I'm getting psyched, too."

It seemed the next week Floyd would be celebrating his thirtieth birthday by surfing Hamburger Lane at daybreak, in front of the legendary Charlie Kemp, cover photographer for *In Da Tube* magazine.

Hamburger Lane was the narrow alley between Cow's Head Point and a towering rock column out to the right. It was two miles south of Sherwood Beach. What made this narrow lane of ocean so worth staying out of ' was the old wreck of the steamship *Arbitrator*. Massive Pacific swells would get tripped up on the wreck's hull, just ten feet underwater, and explode between the point and the rock. If you wiped out in there, the tons of water pressure per square inch wouldn't be a laughing matter. The story was that the only guy to have ever tried surfing it—it was years ago, but everyone remembers he was a real maniac—thought it would land him on an anniversary cover of *Stoked*. He was lucky, though: He limped out of Sherwood General with a patch over one eye and a pickle jar that contained the shattered cartilage from his left knee.

Part of the unwritten surfer's creed is never to tell another surfer what he should or shouldn't surf. But in the early morning of Floyd's thirtieth birthday, I sprinted over to Floyd's shop to violate that creed, while Doug, probably in his warmest aloha spirit, was out persuading Charlie Kemp to pack up his tripod and leave Hamburger Lane.

TURNING chunks of featherweight polyurethane foam into movie rocks was a dream job for Floyd Miller because nobody cared when he put in his forty hours. With the key Floyd kept on a lanyard around his neck—the same neck not long ago needing seven stitches—he could let himself into the rock shop nights, leaving his days free for surfing. On Floyd's thirtieth birthday, it was a relief to find his surfmobile still parked outside the shop at five o'clock in the morning. See, my station wagon was back in surgery at the garage, and I'd had to zip on my jogging suit in a panic and sprint over after the alarm on my supposedly waterproof-sandproof wristwatch had startled me—twenty-eight minutes later than it was supposed to. I wasn't about to miss what might be my last chance to have a talk with Floyd.

Right after Floyd had bought his surfmobile—a secondhand taxi the California sun had bleached to a pale lemon—he'd driven it onto Sherwood Beach, where I'd helped him pry off the rear window. Many summers later, at dawn, there I was sliding through that slot and into the backseat, directly behind the driver's position.

The biggest surfboard in Floyd's arsenal was over my right shoulder, lying upside down through the right half of the taxi. Its nose was propped up on the dash, just above the glove compartment, while the middle rested on top of the front seat and the tail section hung straight out over the trunk, bottom fin aimed toward the few still-visible stars. I sat there watching the taxi's familiar silver-and-black interior grow lighter until my watch's alarm—it sounded like an angry electric bee—startled me again. When I finally stopped it, I flopped down over the sand on the backseat to relax until Floyd showed up. I wasn't sure what exactly I was going to say to try to change Floyd's mind about surfing Hamburger Lane. A cobra looked down at me from the low ceiling Floyd's surfboard made above my head. I pulled the visor of my baseball cap toward my chin until I saw only little circles of light made by the eyelets on top. The gulls were definitely getting louder.

I hadn't planned on becoming a surprise for Floyd. But when I woke up in Floyd's backseat, the surfmobile was already accelerating over what sounded like the gravel fill on the fake-rock shop's parking lot. I was going to raise my head out from under the surfboard immediately and say hi to Floyd, but then I didn't. It's a weird feeling to be in a confined space with someone who doesn't know you're there, and I guess I just wanted to experience it for a few seconds longer. I could see Floyd's hair and right ear and the stitches running down his neck, but no more. When the surfmobile hit what felt like the smooth freeway to the ocean, Floyd stepped on it, snapped on the radio, and started singing along with the Rolling Stones in a real exaggerated and cool manner, like I guess anybody might when they're alone, or think they're alone. If I had sat up then, Floyd would really have been embarrassed, and I regretted not getting up before, in the shop's parking lot. For one second, I actually considered saying "This is God, Floyd. Stay away from Hamburger Lane." But I was afraid *any* sudden sound occurring some two feet behind Floyd might startle him, and you don't want to do that to someone going sixty miles an hour with you in his backseat. So

I lay as still as I could. That awful alarm on my watch went off then, and Floyd "B-Positive" Miller jerked around, shocked to see a person getting up behind him. We veered out of our lane, bounced off the side of an empty horse carrier being pulled by a Winnebago, and slammed into a patch of impact-absorbing drums that blasted sand when they cracked.

I limped out of Sherwood General a few mornings later with my left ankle in a cast and some soreness all around. The real pain, though, came from what I'd accidentally done to Floyd. That's the permanent ache. Doug tried to make me feel a little better about it, telling me stuff like it wasn't really my fault, and that Charlie Kemp, that jerk of a photographer, had refused to budge from Hamburger Lane anyway. But Doug's still the only one besides me who knows the whole story of the accident. I didn't know how to explain it to the sole living member of Floyd's family, his sister, Tina, a former Miss Malibu—even though I had the chance. Someday I will. She walked into the surfboard shop eventually, carrying the black pouch containing the ashes of Floyd and his big-gun surfboard. The next day, once Doug had persuaded the taco stand's manager to let us turn his speakers toward the waves, the regular Sherwood Beach crowd—it even included shy soul surfer Sue Kyber, whose feet are too wide to fit into any commercially manufactured shoe—paddled out together in a long funeral train, under mostly sunny skies, into sparkling four-foot Sherwood. After I'd scattered Floyd's ashes over the water, there was a minute of silence. Then everyone joined in a long, exhilarating surf session. When one of us caught a good ride, we all hooted and whistled, and when one of us wiped out and went flying into the white water, everyone laughed.

Trying to fall asleep in my hammock that night, I kept seeing Floyd's ashes vanishing into the ocean. Then I got to thinking how all the waves we'd surfed that day had vanished, too, and how the wakes our boards had left in those waves had disappeared along with them, and how even our footprints on the beach had probably been erased by now. So there wasn't really any lasting trace of what we'd all experienced that day at Sherwood; I couldn't recall seeing any surfing-magazine photographers out there documenting us, either. And I decided that to keep paddling out again tomorrow and the day after and the day after that, in the face of all that not really permanent stuff, actually took some courage, too. Maybe not the fifteen-foot-wave variety, but there was still something pretty death-defying about it, and *that's* what I wished I'd had a chance to tell Floyd that morning in the surfmobile.

Peacekeeper

My first month in the Nevada desert wasn't half-bad. Not bad at all, really. The three-hundred-and-thirty-five-ton Peacekeeper-missile transporter—Dad, we call it—was still something pretty different, and a real kick to circle the track in. It would just be me listening to top ten in Dad's air-conditioned cab up front and a ninety-five-ton Peacekeeper resting in back—yeah, that ninety-five-ton guy we call the Kid. Authority, real authority, circling the fifteen-mile oval track at fifteen miles per hour. Me, Dad, and the Kid—a powerful package, really. Listening to stuff like REO Speedwagon. And circling again. And again. Circulating the Kid around the track until my shift is over and the next guy, Tom, shows up for his turn with Dad.

Now, I'm ready to explain this second month, but first you have to understand the way things work around here. See, the Kid can be anyplace. Or maybe I should say he can be in any one of a *number* of places. That's the beauty of the thing. You've got twenty-three heavy-duty shelters spaced out around the track—deep, dark underground-parking-garage-sort-of setups that the Kid can be launched from as soon as you hear the Word. And you've got that huge metal canopy over the back of Dad, covering the Kid. So those spy satellites can take all the home color movies they want, and still—for all the Russkis would know—the Kid could be hanging out in shelter number 2 or in number 19 or in number 5 or on Dad's back heading for number 10, or in any of the other places. So just how are the Russkis going to take out the Kid when they haven't the slightest as to where he is? That's their problem, and they're not going to solve it all by just landing the *muy largo* one in the middle of everything. I mean, they didn't exactly scrimp on materials when they built these shelters, plus there's a generous half-mile between every one of them, too. Sure, they could try to throw up something against *every* shelter around the track and probably take out our lone Kid that way, but that's a lot of wasted ammo when you're left to deal with another hundred and ninety-nine tracks like this scattered around every other desert out here. They'd never be able to send up that quantity—the kind of quantity they'd need to deal with another hundred and ninety-nine wandering Kids. Of course, wouldn't it be just like those loco Russkis to go for it anyway? You know it. But they're only going to end up spoiling it for everybody, if that's their attitude.

Granted, this driving and stopping, driving and stopping is just a big game. You just pick a number, 1 through 23, and as you make your rounds you drop the Kid off in that particular shelter and then keep circling.

At first you just pull something out of thin air, for no particular reason. But then you get to feeling responsible for picking a number with at least *some* meaning. Like your birthday is coming up on the sixth, so you aim straight for shelter number 6. Or one of your kids just turned five, so you aim for shelter number 5. After a while, you've used up all your obvious figures and you find yourself driving into number 21, because maybe the Rams put that up on the board Sunday. And then you'll make 23 your next stop, because that's what the Broncos scored to beat the Rams and cause you to lose a quick ten, and there's your next stop. There's no way the Russkis are going to figure out a system like that. They probably don't even follow pro ball, but, see, even if they did, or even if they *somehow* figured out the Kid's whereabouts and then right away sent one up against you and the Kid, there, say, in number 10, you'd right away get the Word and still have something like half an hour to drive on over to a safer place, like 3, where Tom, bless the guy, stocks the beer and great summer sausage in a little fridge. Personally, I don't think there's a man driving a shift here who'd be able to pass up that possibly final comfort of the beer and great summer sausage waiting in number 3 after hearing the Word.

This second month has gotten a lot tougher. *Much* tougher—and if you don't believe it, ask the guys working the other shifts and you're going to hear the same thing. I mean, *you* crawl around the same track for eight hours a day at fifteen per and see how long the desert scenery holds your attention. *You* try staring down the track all day and see if the track doesn't begin to stare back at you. You're moving down the track, right? No, after a while—

for all you know—you're standing still and the track is moving toward you. Like some video game. Day in, day out, it's the same track with the same view at the same speed with your foot on the accelerator pedal at the same angle while in the same gear with the same old AM on, and on and on it goes.

I've really got to hand it to Tom, though. Tom seems to be enjoying the routine, no problem, even this second month. Of course, he used to drive some pretty hot cargo through densely populated areas. I forget *what* exactly, but Tom said they always had a strict smoking ban along the route, enforced by a whole squadron of motorcycle cops. Anyway, I think that experience has a lot to do with why Tom's handling the job so well now, but if you ask him, he'll give all the credit to an inspirational radio show he listens to while taking Dad on the rounds. And I know that 10 percent of his paycheck goes right to some Fort Worth preacher.

Anytime I feel too sorry for myself, I think about Kasey. He's the night driver on Dad I relieve each morning. Here's a guy who's spent years smoking dragsters down a quarter-mile track in something like ten seconds. And now he's stuck here in the desert, driving old Dad around in circles at an even fifteen mph. In the dark, too. I mean, at least I never before felt any fantastic acceleration or got to enjoy such high-speed thrills. And while I seem to be keeping my own head screwed on pretty well, I'm really wondering about ol' Kasey. Because he's started telling me these odd things when he crawls out of Dad after his shift, all groggy, and I'm there all wired up, thanks to black coffee, and ready to climb in. He's told me about the voices he keeps hearing around number 15, and about the prairie dog family he feeds that lives in 6, and about the way the wind whistles over both 19 and 20 in what he claims are different but harmonious pitches. And one of his latest comments was about a series of those old Burma Shave signs he swears he can see around number 9 just before sunset when everything is so phantomlike:

A guy who drives
Dad wide open
Ain't hardly movin'
He's only pokin' . . .

If the Russkis should ever get wind of Kasey's imagination, they're never again going to have to worry about when would be a *buen tiempo* to fool everyone. Really, it's one thing for Kasey to be out there all night and imagining Mr. and Mrs. Prairie Dog, but something else again when I arrive to take over for him in the early morning and he can't remember where he's left the Kid. "Must be in 10," he'll say, wiping sleep out of his eyes. "No, 8 maybe. Well, *some* even number, I think. Try 20 and 22 before you do a house-to-house. Really sorry, man. Hey, have you ever noticed those things like scarecrows around 17? I bet the Kid's in 17! Yeah, just look for the scarecrows."

It's been at these moments that I've almost found myself wishing the Word would come through. I just hope it doesn't come through during Kasey's shift. And that the Russkis never find out how much our fridge in 3 means to us. Because it's like I said: There isn't a man driving the Kid around here who, after hearing the Word, would pass up that possible final comfort of the beer and great summer sausage waiting in number 3.

Course, maybe we shouldn't let the fridge get so comfortable in any one place. I mean, maybe it's time to start circulating our fridge now, too. Yeah, keep the fridge circulating, keep the Russkis guessing.

Come Stay with Us

Affordable Vacations with the Farm Families
of Beautiful Luling Peninsula

SPLINT'S HOLIDAY
HOMESTEAD

WE are an abstaining family willing to share our fore-fathers' century-old country home with travelers out our way. We strongly encourage you to partake in the day-to-day operation of our bountiful cattle farm. Activities here include branding livestock, haying, and firewood produc-tion. Ambitious guests may want to join our sons (Noah, thirty-eight, and Joshua, thirty-six) as they check their trap lines. Bring along lots of old clothes, steel-toed boots—we have barbed-wire-resistant work mitts to loan you. Waterproof socks a must. Be prepared to participate in the birthing of calves. Steak suppers, our specialty. No better apple-pie-doused-with-hot-fruit-sauce on the penin-sula. Decaffeinated coffee is always on. Recently remodeled guest room contains a large library of inspirational books. Fall visitors witness to the most color this side of heaven. Our boys okay about meeting bus, if necessary. We ask that guests refrain from using perfumes and colognes in our home. No picture taking. Minimum stay, two days. Prepare to enter into the most fulfilling life-style Luling offers. Bright orange clothing brings added peace of mind. WHO WE ARE: Hort & Marliss Splint. WHERE WE ARE: Planted by the Almighty at the geographic center of the peninsula. Eight miles due north on County Road 39. Turn at the Gaddis Sawmill sign. Go four miles west. After "One-At-A-Time" suspension bridge, look for a Gulf station with a telephone outside. Call us for directions.

PRETTY PERFECT
COUNTRY ACRES

COME! Flee the city and choose our historic little cottage as your home away from home. (We thank you in advance for your patience during our restoration.) We operate a thriving egg business and maintain a large herb garden. Our children (Jack, seventeen; Terrence, fifteen; Ginny, thirteen; Neil, twelve; Malc, ten; Marco, ten; Joannie, eight; Tyrone, six; Ben, five; Prink, three; and Shung Chi, one) are always eager to have company. Once the gang has initiated you on their "Tarzan swing" (Luling's only), they'll want you to get better acquainted with all our farm animals, sometimes at very close range. Moonboots, our friendly Asian collie, loves strangers. You will meet, pet, and feed Kong and Mighty Joe, the big twin goats born last Thanksgiving; Sonny and Cherry, the pigmy goats; and Fran, the miniature black mule—all while Tuffy the Shetland pony looks on. A short llama ride away, you'll peek in on our rabbitry, watch the bees make us honey, and explore the caves where the turkey vultures nest. Also on hand to greet you are our clannish barn cats, two unpredictable peacocks, deer, a raccoon who's set up shop in the old Maytag, an ostrich, a people-loving buffalo, and a box of baby rattlers! Gruffy, our black Lab, has been with us for ages, but it won't take him long to warm up to you, too. Meals will start to make you aware of the benefits of quality "whole" foods. Nobody else on Luling can make apple-pie-doused-with-hot-fruit-sauce quite like us. Don't be too surprised if the eldest ones in our brood want to entertain you on their motorized bikes. Grandpa has his workshop in the yard. He loves to tell stories. Some of our favorite nighttime activities include stargazing, collecting fireflies, and water fights. Of additional interest is our talent at taxidermy. Kyle just finished a tableau of comically posed small animals called "The Pardon Came Too Late." No other stay on Luling will compare with yours here! Mother Nature has endowed our acreage with beauty of the highest order. (Swamp walks guided, if preferred.) YOUR HOSTS: Kyle & Brenda Fisk. HOW TO FIND US: Easy, since we're at the exact geographic center of the peninsula. Drive north on Ten Curves Road till fruit stand. (Use low gears.) Bear right on winding gravel road. Twenty minutes later begin lookout for an orange school bus with a blue roof rack. That's our front yard. Remember, *we* are the prettiest and perfectest way to experience Luling Peninsula.

DIETER AND VELMA'S
LAZYBONE RETREAT

COME please liven our big home. Velma and myself immediately consider you family and serve out Luling's best home cooking—much of it as you eat. We're a modest, many-treed hobby farm. On a lone cliff over the blue ocean. Scenery on the peninsula doesn't go getting better since our sunsets come straight off Hollywood. Children we love (ours grown and flown) and have done well especially with honeymooners. We sneak to arouse you for a six o'clock hearty country breakfast. French toast, Luling bacon, wiener schnitzel, hickory oatmeal, Johnson cakes with fresh maple syrup, bread, scones, muffin, jam, jelly, butters, cheese, and watermelon pickles. So have it good while sharing with Velma her interest in local history and genealogy. Afterwards we'll be glad then to give some tips for you to hike up nearby on the Dubenski Incline. But you may rather snooze the morning with us. Beneath the oldest maple on the peninsula. English lunches with roast beefs, Yorkshire pudding, gravy, vegetables from our patch, baked potatoes, cabbage rollouts with Velma's special sauce—you try it!—and fresh dairy milk all you can pour. Big ravine down to the sea is your magnificent thing for walking off lunch. Or prefer to nod out with us in Hansel & Gretel porch swings left over from child days. Dinners served up from the blue ocean—Ahoy! Creamed scallops, scrod crepes, fried-squid casserole. Dessert . . . well, Velma's apple pie doused on with hot fruit is a local myth. Evenings spent back around our opened fire pit. With stories and laughter over the day's adventures, know any good yarns of sailing? We love music, so when you play a instrument by every means BRING IT!! It might just lead to family sing-alongs, then time for s'mores and our too hot cinnamony apple cider. Don't retire to your alpine suite before homemade fudges and ice cream. Then pour down yourself delicious cocoa or eggnog. Other things are golf-carting to the hammocks or catching winks in the little red caboose I built then for my children. Take Velma's party-mix canister beneath the stairs and sleep before satellite TV in your room. If you're thinking around Luling, think of us FIRST. WE ARE: Dieter and Velma Vande-Dor, your host family at your Lazybone Retreat. TO GET TO US: We'll be a ways from all the commotion, get off the north shore highway, beyond once it goes west. Just before County Road 39 falls south we are, but too far if you're seeing the landfill sign. Come on then! No finer breathtaking of the geographic center of Luling exists than you'll have from our dining table.

So What Are You Going to Do <u>Now</u> If You're a Friend of Jim's?

F ROM my spot at the beginning of the assembly line, I can grab on to the metallic-flake counter in front of me, lean back until I'm balancing on just two legs of my stool, and turn and see the guys working all on down the line. I can see each guy in his position, right on down to Jim, who's the tiny shape working at the very end of the line.

Lately, though, when I'm taking it all in like this, Jim hasn't been anywhere in sight. And then I know it's like a sure thing he's snuck back to the break room again, to console himself with a hot one, takes cream and six sugars. Yeah, poor Jim took last week harder than anyone else on the line. And, of course, we all spent a couple of late nights tossing down a few and feeling sorry for ourselves. But it's poor Jim who's even now using *Lucky*'s in place of sleep.

What happened last week was the notice on the break-room bulletin board from the higher-ups. And the tricky thing about reading this notice was that it started out making you feel pretty good. Or at least secure. Back when our line first got together to assemble whammies, the higher-ups couldn't even guarantee we'd still be working the next week. But then the whammy took off. It soared, and became America's number one leisure-time plaything, virtually overnight, and has been the company's bread and butter ever since. So last week's break-room notice from the higher-ups started off in inspirational enough fashion, with this great skyrocketing "Whammy Sales" graph, followed by news of the "key personnel" raises in store for everyone on the whammy assembly line. Sounded great. But then, dammit, came the bombshell, the part that didn't make you feel so good after all, the "New Assembly Line Travel Policy" part. Basically, this policy said we were too important a group of guys, too "key" an assembly line, ever to risk traveling together again. Traveling together to anyplace; traveling together anyhow. The higher-ups apparently didn't want to risk a situation in which one freak travel accident—say, metal fatigue in a plane's horizontal stabilizer—could wipe out their entire whammy assembly line. Not after all the care they'd taken to train us to make the whammies just *so*. And not after the whammy had become the focus of American leisure-time activities.

Well, nobody expected anything like that. Who could have called it? Not me, and not even Phil, the guy next to me on the line who seems to have a guardian angel when it comes to betting on Little League games and who's just had his shoe rebuilt to fill in for the five toes, by the way. Nobody could believe what they were trying to take from us. I mean, they were trying to take the big one away from us. We've always shut down the whole line for the entire Labor Day week and taken our annual fishing trip to Lake Aska. On the bus with all the dark glass. Together. Always. And we were all of us excited and as good as packed for Lake Aska again this year. Until last week, that is, when the notice appeared and guys right away started unpacking, started untying their fancy new trout flies and bass poppers, started mumbling something about to hell with job security and something else about quitting the line, but didn't take any immediate steps in that direction.

And yeah, poor Jim was one of the first of them mumbling. Here's a guy that . . . well, we all came from the bottom, but Jim had done some crawling just to reach that. I mean, here's this guy who used to eke out his existence via these war medals he'd melt down on his stove and take to this guy—Artie, I think his name was. Lord knows that was no haven of job security. And yet here's the same guy thinking of going back to all that now. Thinking seriously of chucking his present job security rather than staying stuck here on the whammy line with no chance of another big fishing trip and plenty of chances of losing another index finger.

Well, at first I was damned if I knew why Jim seemed to need our old fishing trips together so badly. It couldn't have been the fishing itself. Jim usually hauled a few out of Aska, but he always drowned more than his share of artificial lures, too. No, Jim didn't really seem to be in his element on the trips until he'd get to fooling around with his camera and taking those funny shots with us guys where we'd hold up stringers full of minnows we'd put on.

But now I'm realizing that that was just it. That was a big part of his needing the old trips. It was him and the guys, the guys and him. It was the sense of togetherness, the feeling of camaraderie on those trips, that he'd miss now. Of course, I don't want you to think he was one of *those* guys, if you know what I mean. No way. He liked women just as well as the next guy, but he just had this extra thing for getting together with the guys, which Phil tells me is related to his being dropped by this girl—Betty, I think her name was. It seems this Betty was some kind of con artist or other, but Jim was just gone over her, even let her wear his medic-alert bracelet around, but where did it get him? He lived like a pauper while putting her through the first year of law school—three years it took— only to have her gallivant off with this guy who operated a rare-bird hot line, and then go into some business-related field involving unsealing sealed bids and then sealing them back up again. Dropped? Poor old Jim was blind-sided the way it looks now, with only us whammy assembly guys and the fishing trips together giving him the boost and keeping him on his feet.

SO WHAT are you going to do? What are you going to do *now* if you're a friend of Jim's and you want to keep him on the line and away from a lonely existence over a stove hot enough to melt down a Congressional Medal of Honor? Well, you could get the guys together. You could get the guys together and then maybe get each of them to do maybe not so hot a job at their positions on the line. Maybe overdo the enamel bath, deepen one of the grooves, flair out the base ever so slightly. Maybe get the whammy's popularity to tail off after its quality has done the same thing. Then maybe see those of us on the whammy line become less important—more replaceable—again. And then maybe see the whole Assembly Line Travel Policy get lifted, and then *finally* maybe live to see some more sunsets with Jim up at Aska, where fresh bait, a cold six, and some companionship with the guys are all you need to sustain life. Definitely worth a try if Bob's idea doesn't pan out. Bob, who works down next to Phil and who lost the earlobe, is certain that introducing Jim to his sister, Lynnette, will help Jim forget about the Aska trips altogether.

I've got my doubts, though, about that little match ever working out. And it's not like Lynnette's another Betty, either. No, she's a world apart from Betty, which sort of turns out to be the problem, really. I mean, it's starting to look like she's a world apart from just about everyone. You add it up: the extra vertebrae, the absence of any need to sleep, all the extra attention from children and small animals, the steering clear of electrical appliances, and, of course, all those doodles involving a multi-mooned planetary environment. No, Jim needs the benefit of her company like I need another injury to my left hand. So my idea, anyway, is to invite Jim to tag along with me and the wife and the kids on one of our next weekend excursions. That may be just what the clinical psychologist ordered. I mean, there's a sense of togetherness, a feeling of camaraderie—family camaraderie—on those weekends that will be just the medicine for poor old Jim. It'll be just Jim and us, us and Jim. And we'll all drive down to the great big theme park together where the kids always use up their whole ticket books riding the Ionosphere

Coaster over and over; laughing after they've breathed in the free oxygen in the on-deck circle on top, and then competing with their little transistor radios while they're getting strapped in to see who can pull in the most distant station. And then we'll swing on over to Indian Echo Caverns and let Jim take some of those funny shots of the kids where it looks like they're holding up those giant Comanche Tear stalactites on their fingertips. I mean, I like Jim, so it's worth a try.

The Gene Norman
Collection

WELCOME to the story of the Gene
Norman Collection. I'm going to tell you this story as best
I can. And I'd better tell it to you now, before I hear any
more of the conversations going on in a diner over my
kitchen radio and get all distracted. Because while I'm still
about 90 percent the same old Gene Norman, nonunion
plumber, serving as curator of the Gene Norman Meteorite
Collection over this past year has put a good 10 percent
of me on the fritz.

It was about a year ago that my meteorite collection began. And, yeah, it hurt back then when Helen, my
dear wife who I miss so much now, called me a knuckle-
head for spending all that time with it. But after the first
week of name calling, guess who began coming out to the
carport just as soon as the last dinner dish was in the rack
to join the knucklehead and his meteorites? Those sure

were the days. Every evening Helen and I would drag that bench I made out of old drainpipes and faucet parts from the porch to the carport. Then, while my meteorites just lay there on the concrete floor in front of us, we'd sit back and share a bag of barbecue-flavored potato chips. Yeah, those three meteorites were better than TV. And to sit and stare at them, together, was . . . well, relaxing in a funny sort of way.

After five weeks of togetherness, though, something happened to Helen. She suddenly developed her remarkable healing ability, jumped into rehearsals with a guitarist and a keyboard man and an eight-voice choir with glow-in-the-dark hymnals, and then went out on the road in the Helen Norman Crusade. She told me it was something she just all of a sudden *had* to do. But I haven't heard from her since. And not to start sounding jealous now, but she can't exactly heal anyone. Like if, for example, your left shoulder had always ached to where you thought your whole arm was going to drop off, Helen really only had whatever it took to transfer that pain down to, say, a knee of your choosing. Which was still enough to get her booked into the tri-state Beef Festival at nine hundred dollars per show plus expenses—at least according to a conversation I overheard at the diner between two men who'd signed her up.

Of course, I wasn't there at the diner when I heard them. (I'm still not even sure where this diner is.) See, I was alone in the kitchen at the time, only days after Helen had gone out on the road. I was eating a five-piece Chicken Delight dinner and getting good and depressed about Helen leaving me. And the radio wasn't even on. But all of a sudden, there comes those two guys over it, and they're eating and talking about Helen, loud and clear. Well, what else could I do? I tried to talk to them. I said I was Gene Norman, right into the speaker of my radio, and to please pass the word along to my wife, Helen, if they could, that her husband, Gene, misses her plenty and that he keeps her old apron tied around his waist under his overalls to remind him of the scent of her roast chicken and that he says to *please come home soon.* Then, as I listened, one of the big shots laughed and said to the other, "Talk to her, Nash. Ask her out. She's a real doll, she heals, and I don't believe she's even married."

"Yes, she is!" I screamed into the radio. But they just started ordering blackberry pie and coffee from a waitress. And so I learned that my remarkable new ability to overhear the conversations going on in a diner over my kitchen radio was going to have its limitations; at least there'd be no talking back.

But what, you have a right to ask, makes a person start collecting these unpredictable chunks of interplanetary debris in the first place? Well, most evenings, sitting alone out in the carport now, if I'm not nodding off, I'll stare at my meteorites and search for an answer to that. All I can tell you so far is that they make me feel *special.* Way more special, in fact, than I've ever felt just being Gene Norman, nonunion plumber. I mean, these things probably got flushed out of some asteroid belt a thousand light-years away, and yet somehow they've found their way straight down into *my* collection. I guess they've just gotten into my blood. Of course, to analyze it any further or deeper than that might be to destroy that most beautiful part of me that makes me *me.*

Now, if by this point your curiosity about meteorite

collecting hasn't been really aroused, feel free to just tape this to the mud flap of some truck. I, Gene Norman, sure couldn't hold it against you. Wouldn't it be one dull planet if everybody wanted to collect the exact same thing?

My first meteorite found me early on that special evening one year ago. I was driving home in my van, feeling pretty depressed about myself. I'd just come out of yet another meeting of the Plumbers Local 52, and *again* I'd been turned down. I mean, talk about a tight bunch of jobbety-job jobbers. All of them served together in Patton's Third, what they called the "spearpoint of the spearhead." And lots of them are still carrying around metal. But do you think they'd let old Gene Norman in? No way. And here's me, ship's cook, Korean War, shrapnel from a can of pressurized whipped cream I set on a hot pancake grill still floating around in my neck—only smile with one side of my mouth and *still* can't stand the taste of whipped cream. Why, it's a full-time job just begging to join up with those guys, and next they'll probably create a special new union you'll have to get into just to do *that*. Anyway, I was tooling along in my van and not smiling one bit, when something exploded through the roof. It caved in the glove compartment like tinfoil and ricocheted deep into the springs of the seat next to me. It was a rock the size of a potato, and it looked something like bleu cheese with a sunburn. Boy, what a lousy way that would have been to lose Helen! Now, though, when I'm awake in the carport all night and get to picturing her out crusading with her guitarist, I wonder if I haven't lost her anyway.

My second meteorite came crashing down through the roof one hour later that same blessed night. I was watching Johnny Carson's anniversary special while I tried to recover from my first meteorite. Helen was next to me on the sofa, monkeying around with her wood-burning set. Anyway, just when this opera singer started to show Johnny how to make a breakfast pasta—KAA-RAASH! The missus and I looked at each other and then both of us tore on out to the carport. We thought it was a bomb or something. But then we saw it: the color of Total and the size and shape of a hot-water heater. Only missed the front of my van by maybe the length of a match. Helen and I tried to budge it, but I bet all the plumbers in Local 52 together couldn't have moved it either, and that even goes for rolling it. So we had a nasty hole in the roof of the carport, a big, splintery mess all over the concrete, and smoke pouring out of the living-room sofa, courtesy of Helen's wood-burning tool. But again I felt special, like we'd been selected. That's when Helen called me a knuckle-head. I didn't care, though. I just went and recovered that heavy little potato of a meteorite buried in the passenger seat of my van. And let me tell you, it looked darned good set down next to our big new arrival.

Now, listen: If you don't believe meteorite collecting is for you, don't be afraid to just cook this over your stove for an hour, pour the ashes into an old jam jar half-full of ball bearings, and heave the works into some bottomless lake. It's perfectly okay by me. Maybe you'd be better off collecting something else. I know another nonunion plumber, Ed Ivick, who collects motel soap. Interesting stuff. And I bet owning a tiny bar of soap from a Holiday Inn in New Orleans won't start you healing or hearing conversations over your radio. Still, if any more meteorites find me, you can bet I'll give them a home in my collection.

My third meteorite, the baby, slammed into the suet

feeder in front of our place at 2:18 a.m. on the same night the two others found me. It sounded like a mortar shell and performed like one, too. But I didn't care—I felt so special all over again. Holding a flashlight in my teeth, I was able to pry it out of the ground with a piece of pipe. It was the same color as a bacon and egg-salad sandwich I found behind the refrigerator once, and only about the size of . . . well, you could fit it through the middle of a forty-five, no sweat. After I set it down with the others in the carport, I got comfortable at the kitchen table. A three-meteorite day seemed reason enough to write to the astronomy department of the new junior college upstate. But instead, for I don't know how long, I just sat there and drew my three meteorites over and over. By morning I realized something: I really had been selected. I really was meant to start the Gene Norman Collection. And plumbing would have to take a backseat for a while.

But listen, meteorite collecting wasn't designed for everyone. So don't be afraid to just rip this up now and fold it again and again until you've got something about the size of a Chiclet. Then make a golf ball out of ground beef and stick it in the middle. Then maybe heave it over to your neighbor's German shepherd. Believe me, I'll understand.

You know, before my dear Helen developed her remarkable healing ability and vamoosed, she made me delicious roast chicken. And what do I keep overhearing at the diner every so often now? Only how great their roast chicken is, that's all. And sure it makes me hungry. But what's worse, it reminds me of how much I truly miss Helen, and then, too, of those evenings we spent together sharing our meteorites' company. Of course, then, so help me, I get to picturing her messing around with her keyboard man and wondering if her roast chicken was really all that great in the first place. I really do want Helen to come back home to me, though. I'd even go out on the road and try to find her. But not at the expense of missing some meteorite trying to find me and my collection.

Wayne

I F, on a map, New Jersey resembles a sea horse arched toward the Atlantic, then exactly where the creature's eye would be is where you'll find the town of Wayne. I accidentally found Wayne last week, while driving north on New Jersey state highway 23. There was a big sign saying WAYNE MOTOR INN. Then came the WAYNE AREA CHAMBER OF COMMERCE and the PACKA-NACK WAYNE SHOPPING CENTER, containing WAYNE INTERIORS and WAYNE SAVINGS & LOAN and WAYNE NUTS 'N BOLTS HARDWARE. Then it was THE WAYNE MANOR, along with a smaller sign marking THE WAYNE MANOR ENTRANCE. Soon there was WAYNE TILE AND CARPET, WAYNE DINETTES, and GIANNELLA'S—OF WAYNE. Then, after WAYNE CORK 'N BOTTLE and a skateboard-size sign saying WAYNE ANSWERING SERVICE, came what must be the John Wayne of Wayne signs, a massive WAYNE LINCOLN MERCURY. Following that was a possessive experiment: WAYNE'S MALL. Eventually, there were more and more trees, and less and less Wayne, and some relief from previous Wayne available in signs like KIM'S GEMS and TERRY'S TROPHY SHOP and IKE'S RADIATOR REPAIR. I finally got hit with a WAYNE GLASS—WAYNE CYCLE—WAYNE ELECTRONICS—WAYNE ELECTRICAL SUPPLY barrage. Later, way way beyond Wayne, a blue Chevette pulled alongside me on the highway. I noticed that on the door it said WAYNE MESSENGER, and about all a guy could do then was to hold the wheel steady and marvel at the awesome extent of Wayne.

A Note on the Type

*The text of this book was set on the Linotype in
Garamond No. 3, a modern rendering of the type
first cut by Claude Garamond (c. 1480–1561).
Garamond was a pupil of Geoffrey Tory and is
believed to have based his letters on the Venetian
models, although he introduced a number of
important differences, and it is to him we owe
the letter which we know as "old style." He gave
to his letters a certain elegance and a feeling of
movement that won for their creator an immediate
reputation and the patronage of Francis I of France.*

*Composed by Maryland Linotype Composition
Company, Baltimore, Maryland. Printed and bound by
R. R. Donnelley & Sons, Harrisonburg, Virginia.
Designed by Iris Weinstein.*